Teresa

》》》》》》》》》》　《《《《《《《《《《《

Neera

Teresa

TRANSLATED FROM THE ITALIAN

BY MARTHA KING

NORTHWESTERN UNIVERSITY PRESS
EVANSTON, ILLINOIS

》》》》》》》》》》》　《《《《《《《《《《《

Northwestern University Press
Evanston, Illinois 60208-4210

Originally published in Italian under the title *Teresa* in 1886 by Galli,
Milano. Copyright © 1976 Giulio Einaudi editore s.p.a., Torino. English
translation copyright © 1998 by Northwestern University Press.
Published 1998. All rights reserved.

Printed in the United States of America

ISBN 0-8101-1662-6

Library of Congress Cataloging-in -Publication Data

Neera, 1846–1918.
    [Teresa. English]
    Teresa / Neera ; translated from the Italian by Martha King.
      p. cm. — (European classics)
    ISBN 0-8101-1662-6 (pbk. : alk. paper)
    I. King, Martha, 1928– . II. Title. III. Series: European classics
(Evanston, Ill.)
PQ4730.R2T413   1999
853'.8—dc21
                             98-31619
                               CIP

Chapter I

"Keep up the good work, men."

"We will, Signor Mayor, but it's terrible, and I'm afraid it's going to get worse."

Speaking to the great town* authority was old Tony, the elderly boatman who had seen many floods, and he shook his large disheveled gray head permanently capped by the traditional red beret of Po boatmen.

"We'll do our duty, Tony, and leave the rest to Providence."

Tony didn't reply but went back to work with the other boatmen and the helpers; everyone was busy carrying branches, bags of dirt, broken crockery, bricks, stones to shore up the river.

"Holy God!" exclaimed the mayor, in a half curse, half prayer, as he looked at the rapidly rising river.

The night was black with a threatening sky heavy with rain. It had rained all day, just as it had for thirty-four days.

The stone marking the levels of previous inundations was already covered. The river rose at a slow, relentless pace, with the fierce calm of a monster sure of its prey. It had invaded the low embankment; now it touched the edge of the higher embankment, foaming with a dull roar.

* Though never named, the town is Casalmaggiore, on the left bank of the Po, in the province of Cremona.

The big danger was water destroying the embankment from underneath.

For forty-eight hours it had labored relentlessly, knocking down the trees and old houses closest to the river, those in greatest peril. The inhabitants of these cottages, almost all poor, fled with household goods—and they were not yet on safe ground when the pickaxes of the masons could be heard on the walls, making the debris rebound in the dim light of the lanterns held by boys.

An octogenarian, whose bed was being carried to a more secure place, went up to the men who were holding that poor worm-eaten piece of furniture and said to them with tears in her eyes: "Throw it in, too. Anyway, I won't be able to sleep there tomorrow."

"Yes, throw it in," the mayor said. "I'll get this poor woman another one."

The old woman's bed immediately disappeared into the greedy waves that kept rising.

The subprefect and the lieutenant of the carabinieri came from the woods where they had gone to inspect the safety of the banks.

"What do you think?" the mayor asked as soon as he saw them.

"No danger for the moment. How is it here? Are they afraid?"

"There was a bit of commotion when we ordered them not to go to bed tonight, and to be ready when they hear the bell."

"Of course!"

The subprefect—a handsome, elegant Southerner, with the face of a romantic—ran his right hand through his hair, rearranging it with a habitual drawing room gesture. At the same time he looked at the dark mass of people, almost all gathered beside the embankment, forming various fantastic, anxious groups, among which resin torches ran like will-o'-the-wisps. Then he leaned closer to the lieutenant and murmured in his ear, with lively gestures:

"But tell me if it was sensible to build a town in this position, with water above it! Behind the embankment the ground slopes at a frightening angle, and down there, that hole where they've built their damned town seems just like a glass ready to drink a toast."

The lieutenant, a calm Piedmontese, was struck dumb. Unsure how to reply to the brilliant but inopportune observations of his superior, he confined himself to a noncommittal, "Uh-huh!"

People ran in every direction, whimpering, cursing, questioning each other, bumping into each other, pushing ahead without apology, without regard for each other.

The two engineers sent by the government were besieged with questions, opinions, suggestions.

They answered, "Yes, yes," quickly, leaning over the river, testing with their feet the resistance of the river at the weakest points.

"What level do we have, Tony?"

"It's come up another half inch," the boatman replied, bending his large gray head and holding a match over the stone.

A discouraged moan snaked through the crowd. Someone who had not understood demanded: "What? What?"

"It's come up another half inch."

A group of women surrounded the mayor: "Signor Mayor, if you would allow a procession in honor of San Giovanni Nepomuceno who watches over water and has performed miracles . . ."

The subprefect interrupted: "What are these women doing here? No women here. Go home. And children? Children too? No children here. Go away, away, away. Go home."

The mayor calmed him down by saying quietly: "What can they do in their houses? They can't even lie down this wretched night!"

"That's true. That's true. But I can't stand women. They make me nervous."

"Ooh! . . ."

"In certain cases, I mean, like this." He took his secretary by the arm. "Luzzi, send Minister S.E. a telegram immediately. Tell him money's needed because the river keeps rising and the people are demoralized."

The secretary took off running.

"Luzzi!" He called him back. "Add that the authorities are on duty, giving encouragement and help."

A small man, shoulder high to the mayor and the subprefect, dressed in black and wearing a leather skullcap, approached the authorities.

"The monsignor sent me to see if his presence is required . . . to tell the truth his rheumatism is bothering him . . ."

"Tell the monsignor to stay where he is!" the subprefect replied. "He should take care of his rheumatism. We need strong arms here more than prayers."

"Yes," agreed the mayor in a conciliatory tone. "It's useless for him to endanger his health. Give him my respects and tell him to pray for everyone."

"And listen for the bell!"

The little man in black disappeared into the crowd.

"Who was that?" one of the engineers asked the lieutenant.

"He's the monsignor's servant."

"And the monsignor?"

"He's Monsignor Capperi, the bishop who heads our clergy, the one who officiates at solemn feasts."

"How many officials there are in this town!" the engineer remarked sarcastically, and went back to watching the water-washed embankment, the menacing water, and the town stretched out like a condemned man on his death bed.

A cracked voice shouted: "The train track is flooded near Cremona, the trains aren't running."

Everyone looked at the speaker. He was Signor Caccia, the tax collector, a tall, red-faced man with thick shoulders, a strange head with ringlets around his ears, and two arched eyebrows making him look a little like a portrait of Goldoni, but a surly Goldoni.

"Is that right, Signor Caccia? How do you know?"

"I heard the news from my brother-in-law, who arrived from Piadena about two hours ago."

"Yes? And what does he say?"

"It's awful. An entire family drowned on a farm near Bosco: the father, mother, five children, and the wife of one of their sons. They couldn't save anyone."

"Madonna!"

"Marchese d'Arco's land is flooded, the wheat ruined, not to mention the grapes. Fifty farmers' families won't have anything to eat this winter!

"That's not all. Others on the farm would like to know what they'll be eating this winter, too."

A woman asked the collector quietly: "And your wife, Signor Caccia, tell me, how's your wife?"

"You can imagine! . . . She's been in pain all day long."

Someone overhearing asked in turn: "Is your wife ill?"

Signor Caccia arched his eyebrows even more, and murmured, "Uh-huh."

Then the woman remembered. She colored slightly and said grimly, "Poor thing, and on a night like tonight!"

Signor Caccia searched the crowd for the long thin shape of Doctor Tavecchia, and finding him speaking animatedly with the judge, said: "If you can, for a moment, make a brief visit at my house . . . as a friend, you know? . . . For my wife, just to reassure her."

"I'll go, I'll go . . ."

"Oh, it's not urgent. Just for a moment."

Then when he saw Caramella, the cripple who sold cooked apples and pears, pass by on his way to town, he took him by the sleeve. "Are you going home, Caramella?"

"Yes, Signor Tax Collector. Do you need something?"

"Yes, I do. As you pass by my house, go in and tell my wife there's no danger at the moment, she should stay calm; Doctor Tavecchia will come see her . . . Tell her I have to stay here a little longer, just to see how things go."

Caramella limped away.

Suddenly general attention was turned to a black mass flowing down the river by the bank.

"It's dead wood."

"It's a plank."

Something was seen moving, perhaps some poor shipwrecked people driven from their homes, going toward certain death.

"It's a boat," Tony shouted.

"A boat? Impossible. Who could be guiding it?"

"No one. It's adrift."

"Then it's empty."

"No."

"Yes."

Attention became so concentrated no one spoke. They all fought to get in front to see better. The engineers went up the embankment with lanterns, the subprefect and the mayor following them, like everyone else—fearful, curious, trembling. A few women recited the rosary quietly, holding their kerchiefs under their chins, not daring to go too close.

"It's really a boat."

"Call out to it."

"Hey! You there!"

Not one, but a hundred voices repeated: "Hey! You there!"

And all the while the boat came down at breakneck speed. At once ropes and grapples were fixed to help the rowboat, a crude fishing boat, reach the shore.

"Who is that madman?" the subprefect quietly asked the lieutenant of the carabinieri, who shrugged his shoulders.

A man's shape could be distinguished standing in the middle of the boat, struggling fiercely with his oars to keep off the tree trunks the current dragged in its vortex; and all around the river roared, throwing up a turbid yellowish foam to the surface, where rags, pieces of wood, broken furniture, animal cadavers, floated.

"Doesn't anyone know him?" the subprefect turned to ask.

"Yes . . . I think," answered the mayor, hesitating, not entirely sure.

A voice from among the boatmen shouted, "It's Orlandi."

"It's Orlandi, it's Orlandi," they repeated in turn, amazed, full of admiration.

"I thought as much," murmured the mayor, "it could only be him! . . ."

"Orlandi? Someone from town?"

"No, he's from Parma. But everyone here knows him. A complete fool . . ."

"That's obvious."

While the authorities made their uncomplimentary remarks, the fellow's reckless boldness was acclaimed by the enthusiastic bystanders. When the boat touched ground and a soaked Orlandi got out of it, clothes disheveled and hands torn, as jaunty as if he had been on a pleasure cruise, all the boatmen surrounded him, overwhelming him with questions.

Before answering, Orlandi took a bundle wrapped in a woolen blanket from the bottom of the boat and laid it in the arms of the first woman he saw.

"Here's a baby that arrived without your labor."

"Santa Vergine!" the woman exclaimed and gently uncovered the little body.

The women huddled around, kissing him, caressing him, warming his stiff little fingers. Orlandi said he had saved him by a miracle, from a miserable hovel everyone, made cruel and crazy by terror, had abandoned.

"But you, dear Orlandi, do you have such little regard for your life as to endanger it on the river on a night like this?" the mayor questioned him as he came forward.

"I didn't have time to think about it, I can tell you that," answered Orlandi, shaking his proud head and smiling so that in the dim light the whiteness of his teeth could be seen under his little black mustache.

"I've been going around for three days, delivering relief supplies that came in slower than molasses. Never mind, we do what we can. I was down there in the Arese woods when the river broke over the bank and there was no way out. I took this boat, tossed the baby in, and put myself in the hands of God or the devil!"

"Don't curse," the woman who had taken the child dared to say. "It's turned out well, and you must thank Providence . . ."

Orlandi paid no more attention, intent on looking at the terrible flood damage and the men working to shore up the bank.

"Seems it won't go higher tonight."

"God willing!"

The groups began to thin out. The women and old people urged one another to return to their homes. Signor Caccia set off behind the doctor.

The authorities were obliged to remain; and strong young men, including Orlandi, also stayed, inebriated by danger and fatigue. They helped carry sacks, hold torches, and gave a hand with the masons' picks until dawn grew white over the woods, illuminating their pale, dejected faces and the still menacing river. And behind the town, the rising sun also outlined gutted houses that looked like huge, incurable sores.

Chapter II

The tax collector's house was situated in the middle of Via di San Francesco, the so-called high-class street. Signor Caccia wasn't a rich man, but his wife came from a good family and brought the house as part of her marriage settlement when she fell in love with him and wanted to marry him at any cost.

It was a small house with a modestly provincial look compared to the other houses on Via di San Francesco. It was particularly overpowered by the Varisi mansion—dark, imposing, with the windows always closed because the marchesa lived in Cremona, but with a quartered coat-of-arms above the door as if to show the owner was at least present in spirit.

Other mansions, more or less ancient, were lined up on the right and left of the street, which began at the main piazza at one end and was lost in the fields at the other.

The second floor of the tax collector's house was illuminated, and one could divine some movement beyond the lace curtains. In the master bedroom Signora Soave Caccia was settled in an armchair, elbows on the chair arms, quietly complaining: "What a night, Signora Caterina, what a night!"

Signora Caterina, a large, red-faced woman wearing a black tulle cap with orange ribbons, consoled her as well as she could, circling the room while making certain preparations.

"And my husband had to go to the river . . ."

"What do you expect? A man is a man. They're all down there, the subprefect, the mayor, the lieutenant . . ."

"And the bell? Oh, dear, if the alarm bell rings . . . how will we get away?"

"Try to stay calm. Yes, that bell business is a precaution, but it won't happen. Just in case, your husband's there and will have time to make plans. There's no lack of strong arms and people of good-will. Just think, even the singers, those poor singers who came here hoping to have a good season in our theater, well, even they were recruited. The impresario threatened not to pay them if they didn't pitch in; the tenor preferred to run away, giving up his quarter.* But all the others rolled up their sleeves and have been working on the embankment since morning. Carlino's home, isn't he?"

"Oh, yes! He wanted to go to the river, too, but his father wouldn't let him. He's with Teresina. The twins are tucked in bed with their clothes on . . . just in case . . . but what a night, what a night! Oh me, Signora Caterina, I'm so unfortunate."

Signora Caterina stopped in the middle of the room, swaddling band in hand, and assumed a severe look—an imperious, gruff severity that always succeeded in calming her clients: "I tell you it won't help a thing for you to get yourself worked up like this. Don't think about the Po, think about your own business."

Signora Soave answered with a moan, and let her hands slide down to embrace her belly in resignation.

The wife of Signor Caccia was a frail, sickly little woman in her forties, with a long, ashen face palely illuminated by two dull black eyes—calm, good eyes that had cried profusely, that still cried easily, with a sweet, resigned weakness. Never was a name so well suited to a woman. In town when they said "Signora Soave,"† everyone connected that name with the melancholy face of the tax

---

* The rate paid singers by theatrical impresarios.
† *Soave*—"sweet," "soft."

collector's wife. And a tiredness showed in the way she moved, as though she were dragging a long chain. Her speech was brief and hesitant, habitually silent before Signor Caccia's hearty but imperious voice. With no impulse to react, no energy to respond, convinced a woman's primary virtue was obedience. Her hair the color of burnt coffee, parted in the middle, fell down on her little forehead, and often, with a languid movement accompanied by a sigh, she would raise a hand to smooth it. Then a thin little hand as colorless as old wax was revealed, with tight little bracelets of woven horsehair set with a rosette on her wrist.

"It will be exactly fifteen years next month," Signora Soave said after following the course of her thoughts in silence for a bit.

"What's been fifteen years?"

"Since my Teresa was born."

"That's right."

"And the very next year Carlino. Do you remember, Signora Caterina?"

"Do I! We're getting old."

Another silence. "The twins are eight years old . . . I didn't think I'd have any more."

"My! He who goes to the mill gets covered with flour."

"It's God's will," concluded Signora Soave with a sigh.

The big heavy woman began to laugh loudly, making her massive body shake.

"If only it's a boy!" the woman sighed again.

"Carlino's not enough for you?"

"Oh, not for myself. But what can girls, poor things, look forward to in this world? . . ."

The corners of her mouth folded in deep discontent, and her black dull eyes veiled with tears.

"Cheer up, forget those gloomy thoughts. We're women, but,

goodness, no one has eaten us. You've already got three girls, one more, one less . . . this way Carlino won't have to go to the army."

A grave, tormented silence returned, broken occasionally by the suffering woman's moans.

"Look, Signora Caterina, in this room I was born; in this room . . . soon . . . perhaps today, who knows, I may die."

"Do I have to listen to this?" interrupted Signora Caterina, hands on her hips. "Someone hearing you talk like that would think you're a silly little girl, not the mother of four children—five at any moment! Why should you die? You could die just as I could, suddenly, in an accident. Did you hear about what happened yesterday? The mayor's brother, that man who looked the picture of health? . . . In a *Jesus* without even time to say "amen." He was reading a letter, *plop*, he was dead. We shouldn't think about death; it comes when it's time to come. Besides, we women have seven lives, like cats . . . so cheer up. In an hour, an hour and a half at the most, it will all be over. Look, I told my sister-in-law Peppina before I left the house: expect me at sunrise, because Signora Caccia will get it over in a hurry. This isn't the first day we've met, eh! Have a little faith."

Somewhat calmed, Signora Soave gave the room a caressing glance, almost as though finding friends in the two walnut chests of drawers; in the bed half hidden under a beautiful yellow raw silk blanket with large green flowers, the sheets turned back, decorated with a muslin frill; in the prie-dieu covered with books, the knee rest worn from lengthy use; in the small greenish mirror, hung somewhat high, where she could see only her face; in the curtains at the window, embroidered by her own hand, with a bird and palm alternating with a rhombus shape; in the two pictures representing the marriage of the Virgin Mary, framed in black wood.

With the greatest pleasure of all, Signora Soave's glance rested on a small wax baby boy under a glass bell. That yellow baby with two small black spots for eyes above a small protuberance simulating the nose; that baby with a sweet and resigned expression, lying for more than twenty years amid the paper flowers and silver stripes decorating his crib. That naked and holy baby drew tender feelings from the woman, making her melt with love and respect, with a desire to weep, to kiss it, to commend herself to its tiny blessed hands. The grandeur of God represented by that little baby boy struck her with pious, devout awe. She got up and, moving with difficulty, went to place a kiss on the glass bell. Then with hands clasped she stood still, absorbed in sorrowful contemplation.

The door next to the bed slowly opened, and a young girl coming in asked, "Mamma?"

Signora Soave was startled: "What do you want, Teresina? Didn't you go to bed earlier?"

"Oh, how can I? I was at the window with Carlino, waiting for Papa. Caramella passed by and told me not to worry, that right now there's no danger. Papa'll come home soon."

"God be praised! Go to bed, Teresa, go to bed."

"And you, Mamma?"

"I'm going right now."

The girl started to leave, but before the door closed her mother went to her uncertainly, put a hand on her shoulder, and said in a low trembling voice: "Pray for me . . ."

"Mamma . . . Mamma . . ."

Now perfectly calm, with a mysterious and sweet solemnity, she put a finger to her lips: "Tonight you'll have another little baby brother or sister . . . something you'll understand later . . . but you're the oldest, you should know about it. Now go to bed."

She gently pushed her out and closed the door.

In the narrow hall dividing the master bedroom from the girls' room, Teresina leaned against the door frame, frozen, her throat constricted by unexpected excitement.

She was fifteen years old. She had grown up in a tranquil family atmosphere in a quiet provincial town. This was her first year to stay home from school, and in her duties as young homemaker she still felt the uncertainties of inexperience, but she was sure of her mission to help her mother. She was serious and warmhearted by nature.

The few words her mother had just spoken at the door had made a profound impression in the general excitement of that night. She felt she had all at once become a woman—with a sudden premonition of future sorrows, with a new responsibility, with a peculiar modesty mixed with extraordinary sweetness.

At that moment, for the first time, she seemed to recognize her own sex, feeling a languorous wave flowing in her veins never felt before, and in her brain rose a live, sharp curiosity, which suddenly ceased at the flushing of her cheeks.

All of this lasted a matter of minutes, as though the rent veil disclosing the future fell back again. Feeling calm once again, with a more melancholy and intense calmness, she went back into her own room. Her brother was leaning on the windowsill waiting for her. She looked at him with new insight, and when he said something she started at the sound of a male voice, glancing at him hastily, afraid he might be able to read her secret in her face.

But Carlino was thinking only about the flood. He would like to be on the embankment with the others and was leaning out the window to see if someone would pass by to ask for news.

Other windows were open like theirs. Frightened women looked out, trying to catch some news, fearing the bell toll that would warn them to leave.

"You know?" Carlino said, with the slightly silly smile of a fourteen-year-old boy. "Old lady Tisbe has been ready for two hours, with her silverware in her apron and her little dog under her arm."

Teresina didn't laugh.

"If only I could . . ." Carlino went on, throwing one leg over the windowsill. "Just for a minute, just to look. You think I can't climb out the window?"

"Come on, now—that would be the last straw."

She talked to him in a whisper by the window, staring into the darkness. All at once she put an arm around her little brother's neck, bending until her cheek touched his short hair, wiry as a brush.

He was unconscious of the caress. Leaning forward on his arms, looking in the direction of the piazza, he said: "What if it should come roaring down from there! All the way down! What a riot . . ."

It wasn't fear of danger that excited him but the new diversion. The whole river in the town! Ha! . . . He laughed, still thinking of old lady Tisbe with the little dog under her arm and silverware in her apron.

"What a disaster!" Teresina murmured, shivering, hugging the boy close with an irresistible need for tenderness.

"Hey!" he said, shrugging her away. "You're suffocating me."

He wiggled from her embrace with a snort. Humiliated, the girl withdrew to her bed at the end of the room. Sitting on a stool next to the headboard, she lay her head on the pillows. Nearby was the twins' bed, one lying at the head, the other at the foot, dressed, with a shawl thrown over their soundly sleeping bodies.

Soon an unusual coming and going in her mother's bedroom made Teresina sit up and go listen at the door.

Silence. She was about to return to her place next to the bed when a baby's wail made her gasp. And immediately, without reflection, obeying an impulse, she went into the adjacent room.

"Mamma, may I come in?"

Signora Caterina came to the door, looking very serious, with a finger at her lips.

"Let her come in," the voice of Signora Soave murmured weakly from beneath the floral blanket.

Teresina entered on tiptoe, holding her breath with excitement. Signora Caterina showed her a rosy little baby girl, wrapped in a diaper.

"Oh, how little she is!"

She wanted to take her in her arms, but Signora Caterina wouldn't allow it.

"Later, when she's swaddled."

Teresina kissed her head gently. Then, going up to her mother's bed she bent over her reverently, full of tenderness, hiding a sense of fear.

"Leave your mother alone," Signora Caterina said brusquely.

"I'm fine," Signora Soave murmured, returning her daughter's caress with a look, adding: "Teresa is my little helper, she has to be a second mother . . ."

"Yes, yes," the girl replied, so moved she was nearly sobbing.

Without another word, Signora Caterina took her by the arm and pushed her out of the bedroom.

Carlino ran to his sister, shouting: "Here's Papa. Now we'll hear the news. He already told me they've knocked down all the houses near San Rocco."

Teresina didn't understand anything. She had news, too. Pale and trembling, she told her brother: "A little sister's been born."

"Oh, really? I knew it was going to happen." And he ran down the stairs to meet his father.

Teresina remained stock-still, struck by her brother's last words. How did he know?

Chapter III

Panic over the flood subsided. Little by little, the town again took up its chronic calm resignation that saw nothing in the future to smile about. The long, wide streets were again deserted and silent between a double row of closed shutters and high dark walls. The grandiose skeleton of what had been a city, contrasting with the dearth of inhabitants, gave an altogether gloomy cast to everything under that dull Po Valley sky. And in the soft, damp atmosphere along the river bordered by melancholy woods, November was stripping the leaves.

Caramella the cripple, who lived on the edge of town where he had a kitchen garden, was beginning his morning rounds, pushing a wheelbarrow full of cooked apples and pears.

"Oh, beautiful pears! . . . pears! . . . pears!"

Via di San Francesco was entirely deserted and all the houses silent, with something still gloomy and sleepy in the vaporous gray atmosphere.

Leaving his wheelbarrow on the sidewalk, Caramella stopped at the tobacconist's and went in to have a small glass of grappa.

"Winter's trying to come early this year," the tobacconist said, rising on tiptoe to take the bottle from the shelf.

The fruit seller didn't reply at once, concentrating on hiking his trousers higher for warmth. Then he took the little glass and downed it in one gulp, smacking his lips and clicking his tongue.

"Well!" he then said. "The worst winter is always the one around the corner." He cast a glance outside at the wheelbarrow and then at the gray sky. "Don't you want some apples for your little girl?"

"Not today. I'm keeping her in bed and don't want her to eat anything."

Caramella stood in the doorway, his hands in his pockets. The tobacconist came closer, smiling conspiratorially. "You go to the Portalupis' house. Do you know anything?"

"About what?"

"About the second daughter . . . they say the subprefect is courting her."

"Imagine that!" The cripple had nothing more to say. He slowly grasped the handles of his wheelbarrow, and with upturned face kept his eyes on the windows.

The tobacconist watched him go, distracted by other thoughts, until another customer came into his little shop.

"Oh, nice pears! . . . pears! . . . pears! . . ."

Caramella didn't even look at the Varisi mansion. And he didn't look at the house next to it belonging to Calliope, the eccentric misanthrope who made faces like a little urchin behind the iron grating on the ground floor.

Instead he stopped at the judge's house and confidently knocked on the door. Here, in fact, they always bought his pears, because the judge had six or seven little children to send to school, and cooked pears were good for children.

Also at the Portalupis' grand house, the rival of the Varisi mansion, the cripple was welcome; he filled the pantry of the Portalupis, a wealthy husband and wife with three marriageable daughters. Old Tisbe worked for them, a retired maid whom the Portalupis had given two little rooms on the third floor.

Nothing doing with Don Giovanni Boccabadati, Don Giovanni

in name and deed, whose mysterious and questionable life inspired women's curiosity and men's envy.

In the house where he lived alone with an old servant, female shapes could be seen coming and going. Shapes that old Tisbe peered at through her glasses in vain, and the three Portalupi girls looked at with disdain, biting their lips.

Between Boccabadati's house and the judge's was the Caccias' house. The cripple also made a brief stop there since Signora Soave, hearing him coming, would have said to Teresina: "Buy a couple of pears for the twins."

Still half asleep, holding her hair back with her hands, Teresina had sent the servant to the door and she herself stood at the window watching Caramella gently select the pears and put them on the scales—beautiful sweet little smooth-skinned pears golden from cooking, still smoking in a thick syrup.

"Oh, beautiful pears! . . . pears! . . . pears! . . ."

The cripple went down toward the piazza with his wheelbarrow, leaving a wake of good odors, almost like a sweet family warmth, of glowing fireplaces, happy children in stiffly starched smocks: odors and warmth blending into a feeling of well-being, lightly expanding and rising in the austere gray of an autumn morning.

At the window, Teresina followed the wheelbarrow with her eyes, and when she couldn't see it anymore she stood there looking down the long street with its rows of houses: Calliopes' white one, the Varisis' darker one, and the Portalupis', all yellow, with the marble cymas above the windows; the wide, low, rose-colored house where the judge lived with his numerous family; Don Giovanni's mysterious house with green shutters and narrow little door. And then all the others in a row, the irregular line of roofs disappearing in the distance to the right and left against the strip of pale sky.

Teresina felt a prickly shivering on her arms barely covered by a percale gown—not irritating, almost pleasant. And her hair danced on her forehead and neck in youthful disarray, producing a enjoyable tickle, like a caress. When the breeze died down, she shook her head to prolong the simple childish pleasure of that gentle wave across her neck, her eyes continually wandering down the long street, observing with interest the cobblestones interspersed with grass and the two rows of reddish brick sidewalks, sunken in many places.

At the end of the street, the postman came out of the piazza reluctantly dragging his square-toed boots, the black leather bag at his side, a surly expression on his face. In a moment he was gone. Teresina guessed he had gone into the pharmacy. He reappeared, zigzagging across the street from right to left, from left to right, leaving *La Mode nouvelle* for the young Portalupi women and the *Corriere di Cremona* for their father; three letters for Don Giovanni Boccabadati. He went right on past Teresa's house without stopping. He left a large yellow envelope and printed matter at the judge's door, then he crossed the street and lifted Calliope's rusty door knocker.

A vague and ambiguous new feeling came over Teresina: a kind of humiliation and resentment. All those newspapers, all those letters were being brought to those destined for a world of emotions. In the postman's black leather bag were joy, sorrow, hope, elation, promise, curiosity, fantasy, affection—all desirable things unknown to the young girl. Here was life coming from far away, the sympathetic threads joining those separated from each other, the beginning of future adventures, the final word of a hundred ended adventures. In that common bag carried around so indifferently from door to door, a thousand hearts leapt, a thousand interests crossed: business and passions, art and fame, noble sacrifice, subtle vendettas, ignoble cowardice, sacred heroism.

All life's secrets were there. Teresina didn't put all this into words, but she vaguely thought it, with a hidden sense of envy, a surprising greediness rising up in her that instant for the first time, filling her breast with a long, bitter sigh.

Calliope's house remained as closed and silent as a tomb.

In the meantime, leaning against the wall, the postman pulled out letters from the bottom of the bag: long envelopes addressed clearly with businesslike flourishes; neat white envelopes with carefully written addresses on a straight line with the stamp affixed evenly, as a schoolgirl would do; letters enclosed in English envelopes, with thick, pearl-colored, perfumed paper, mysterious; letters with violet ink, and nicely printed wide gold initials, correspondence between women; thick letters badly folded, with ink stains and traces of dirty fingerprints, two lines of writing and four errors.

And a slew of postcards written vertically, horizontally, diagonally: very many words, few, very few, almost none, one word. Circulars, announcements, invitations, pamphlets—all passed rapidly through the expert hands of the postman, who put everything back in the bag, keeping only one letter in his hand and knocking for the third or fourth time on the invincible door.

Teresina did not know Calliope. She had never seen her clearly, only getting glimpses of her through the window grating, her face half-covered by a wide yellow kerchief, talking to herself and swearing at all the men who passed. It had been too short a time since Teresina had grown up for her to consider Calliope differently from the way the town children did: a crazy woman to be mocked. She had heard her story recounted in snatches, with many gaps between one incident and another—gaps that the girl's sober imagination had never bothered to fill.

She knew that from an early age Calliope had been raised almost like a daughter by a contessa. And here she faced the first lacuna, as many people insisted Calliope was really the contessa's daughter—something Teresina thought absurd. But in any case, the contessa had loved Calliope and had her educated by an old priest, she herself filling in the instruction necessary for girls.

At that time the contessa and Calliope lived on a solitary farm, and even then Calliope was known to have strange tastes, going alone through the countryside with her hair flying loose, a little rifle slung over her shoulders: bold, violent, wild. Those few people who had occasion to cross the farm heard her whistling in the poplar woods, imitating birds' songs, and sometimes they saw her running pell-mell through the fields, jumping over bushes, her hands scratched by thorns and her clothes torn.

She had a strong, virile beauty.

Doctor Tavecchia, who once took care of her when she fell from a tree and broke an arm, said she was one of the most beautiful women he had ever seen. The strange clothes she wore emphasized her strong and slender Amazon's body. When she covered her head, it was with a man's wide, black hat. She never wore lace, ribbons, or jewels; her dresses were black or white. Often she would sew fresh flowers around her skirt and make a strange, original headdress of flowers that would have looked awkward on anyone else, but on her was enchanting.

The second lacuna: Teresina had heard mysterious whisperings about a French officer, a flight, a betrayal, and other things she had not understood very well and that had not interested her up to now.

Then there was talk of Calliope the nun. She had been in a convent for two years, the model of humility and penitence. Suddenly, on the eve of her vows, she disappeared.

The third and last lacuna encompassed some fifteen years and led the strange woman—all alone in the world—to shut herself up in that house from which she never came out, and where the town charitably did not disturb her, leaving her in peace with her harmless insanity.

The whole complicated and improbable story came to Teresina's mind while the postman waited. And when the shutters of the only window on the first floor finally opened, and Calliope's wild head appeared in the opening behind the grating, the girl looked at her intensely with new pity.

Teresa didn't have much time to observe her, because after rudely grabbing the letter, the dotty woman immediately shut the window, launching two or three crude invectives at the postman.

Teresina stood staring at Calliope's closed window as though hypnotized, lulled by that common phenomenon where the mind seems to be sleeping while awake.

Below, under the rays of the slowly emerging sun, the street came out from the gray morning fog to enter the bath of light. Some doors opened. Old Tisbe, faithful to her ancient morning routine, hung blankets out the window. From time to time she appeared, scratching her cap, casting suspicious sidelong glances at the house across the way, whose green shutters remained resolutely shut in the sweet, warm isolation of unknown mysteries.

Doctor Tavecchia passed by, a little stooped with the years, in his long dark wool coat with velvet collar. He walked head down, thinking about his patients.

Then the monsignor's cook went by, a coarse, robust, curt woman who seemed like mistress of the whole town and who expected the best goods from shops because, as she said, it was for the monsignor.

Luzzi, the prefect's secretary, passed by—thin and sprightly, wearing a light overcoat of a beautiful blue color, close-fitting at his waist. He looked up at all the windows, turning his head a bit to look at Teresina.

The mayor's wife went by, completely enveloped in a black veil, holding a large puce-colored book with worn edges. She was going to Mass at San Francesco.

With a great clatter, the shutters at the Portalupis' house were thrown open—old Tisbe from the window above immediately hauled in her blankets—and the young Portalupi women appeared one after the other amid the lace curtains, all three showing off pink caps. The resembled each other in a strange way, all three ugly beyond compare. They nodded slightly at Teresina, keeping their mouths pursed, shoulders straight, arms to their sides. With half-closed eyes they struck a noble, dignified pose. They stood a moment leaning on the windowsill—or more precisely on a long padded bed pillow embroidered by their precious hands, and they withdrew one after the other as they had come.

From the judge's door erupted four children, followed by their poor mother, uncombed and in slippers, trying to reassure the smallest, who didn't want to go to school and who was crying like an open faucet.

The sight of the children made Teresina start. And her little sisters? She had forgotten them.

She ran quickly to the twins' bed and found them putting on their stockings backward, quarreling over Caramella's pears because each wanted the biggest one.

She helped them hurriedly dress, washed their faces and combed their hair, had them say their prayers, put the pears and two large pieces of bread in their lunch basket.

"I don't want that bread!"

"Why not?"

"I don't like it."

"And I want cheese with the pear."

"Mamma didn't say you could."

"I want it, I want it . . ."

"Hush, don't shout. Mamma's sleeping. Poor thing didn't close her eyes all night because of Ida. But Ida's very little and can't help it. You have to be good, do you understand? You're eight years old and that's big."

Teresina sent them off to school, cautioning them to be good and kissing them on the cheek with the tenderness of a young mother.

At the window she watched them go off down the street, letting herself fall into an unusual torpor that permitted her to dream while standing on her feet.

»»» «««

Chapter IV

Just inside the Caccias' front door, to the left in the vestibule, were two little steps and a door leading to the tax collector's study. It was a small room with whitewashed walls embellished with sponge-applied spots of blue under chocolate-colored wood molding. The stark simplicity of the furnishing was in keeping with a certain bureaucratic importance, revealed principally by a bookcase of papers enclosed by a wrought-iron grill. This bookcase contrasted with another slightly worm-eaten one with broken glass, half-filled with neatly ordered old books. Against a wall, to leave more space, an old table covered with written and printed papers, a black ink bottle in the middle, two pens, and the tax collector's glasses. Over the table a portrait of the king. Four chairs covered in dark leather completed the furnishings, besides the old armchair shaped like a Roman chariot, where Signor Caccia sat enthroned, often arrogant, always imposing.

Besides the contributors who came at appointed hours to pay the tax collector—who accepted their money with a bureaucrat's superior manner—few people entered the study, and never without a specific reason. In the mornings, Signora Soave would come in timidly to straighten it up a little, taking infinite precautions not to move any papers or change the position of the ink bottle even a millimeter. Precisely at four, opening the door only halfway, Teresina would say from the other side: "It's time to eat." For two hours every day after Carlino came home from school, he would go there with his Latin books and grammars.

Under his father's stern scrutiny he did his homework, obliged to sit perfectly still facing the bookcase, whose books he knew well by their covers. Head in hands, sorrowfully meditating on Virgil and Cicero, he would stare at those books always lined up in the same order: *La Divina commedia, Orlando Furioso, Gerusalemme liberata*—all bound in red leather—a dictionary of fables in sheepskin, two or three other dictionaries, the historical novels *Niccolò de' Lapi* and the *Cimitero della Maddalena, Le Notti* by Young, and Botta's *Storia d'Italia,** the last taking up an entire shelf, twelve volumes the color of chickpeas, unbound.

In the corners there were also some gifts—almanacs, two or three odd books by Walter Scott, *Rimedi securi contro ogni specie di insetti* (*Sure cures for every kind of insect*). However, Carlino saw only the first ones, those august, serious books that contained (according to his father) a great amount of human knowledge. And like a continual threat during the painful hours of homework, they charged him to become a great man also, to write eighteen volumes like Botta, or an extraordinary, thick collection of verse like *Orlando*.

Haughtily arching his eyebrows, Signor Caccia stood looking at his only son, the offspring who had to transmit to future generations the Caccia genius—heretofore unknown. He was convinced that by compelling Carlino to study, Carlino would study; that by compelling him to understand, he would understand; that by compelling him to think, he would think. And he stood over him assid-

---

* *Niccolò de' Lapi,* historical novel by Massimo d'Azeglio (1802); *Le Cimitière de la Madaleine,* historical narration by Jean-Baptiste Regnault-Warin (1800); *Le Notti,* originally *Night Thoughts,* by Edward Young (1742-45); *Storia d'Italia dal 1789 al 1814* by Carlo Botta (1824).

uously, rigorously, terrorizing him with his looks and his rude falsetto voice, making him stick to his Latin studies through fear of physical punishment.

Willy-nilly, the boy reached the fourth year. He proceeded like someone in a crowd, not walking on his own legs, but letting himself be carried by the mass. And he studied and studied, squeezing his head in his hands as long as his terrible father stood looking at him. Except for those times when he got his retribution in the solitary grass-covered lanes where his companions were waiting for him, loafing in the warm noon hours; and in the woods where the stream narrowed to a thread of water, where abundant blackberry bushes grew under the long shadow of poplars.

Opposite the little study where Carlino did his enforced apprenticeship of budding genius, at the other side of the vestibule, was a large, oblong, dark, shabby room, the women's room, where they sewed, ironed, added up the daily expenses. They even ate there, and spent the long winter evenings around an old oil lamp adapted to kerosene. The furniture more or less resembled that in the study; instead of a bookcase, a large wardrobe of white wood, a corner cupboard where bread and leftovers were kept, a table in the middle, a small, angular, uncomfortable divan hard as a rock, several chairs of different shapes and colors. One very low chair was placed on a wooden step below the window. Dominating and overwhelming these modest bourgeois furnishings was a large picture hanging on the longest wall, a massive picture an inch thick in which were hidden the secrets of an ingenious mechanism that moved the windmill arms, the miller's small donkey, and the bell tower clock at the same time.

The timepiece and donkey hadn't moved for a long time, but like a restless ghost the windmill continued to wave its scrawny arms amid the painted trees that formed the background.

Haphazardly lying about were just-begun socks, skeins of wool, diapers, old toys, school notebooks, baskets.

Sitting on the divan with a stool under her feet, still pale and weak from her recent pregnancy, Signora Soave nursed the little one. Teresina came and went with the pap and little clothes, delivering orders and counterorders to the servant in the kitchen. When she was able to rest a minute, she sat in the little chair on the step by the window and continued working.

Her mother looked at her tenderly, worrying about this good daughter of hers. Maybe Teresa would be fortunate! At least more fortunate than she had been . . .

When besieged by these thoughts, Signora Soave would look down at her thin breast where yet another daughter was attached, and feel even sadder.

Signor Caccia avoided this room, and if he appeared by chance, the mother-daughter intimacy was immediately suspended. Both of them would look at him, attentive, fearful of his bad humor, ready to obey his slightest wish.

As soon as he left, the mother would return to her calm, contemplative melancholy, and Teresina, relieved of the nightmare, would smile in the happy serenity of her fifteen years.

Carlino made tempestuous eruptions, frightening his mother, trying his sister's patience, making a muddle of the woolen skeins, raising a mindless uproar, touching everything with his dirty urchin hands.

Peace ended completely with the twins' return from school. Then there was sure to be quarreling. Signora Soave would lose her last remaining energy and raise her dark, dull eyes to heaven, crossing the gray shawl across her chest with a discouraged gesture.

The rebellion lasted until the dinner hour, until Signor Caccia looked around the table with those ferocious looks that struck terror in the entire family.

Afterward, when the tax collector went to the café on the piazza to read the newspapers, the din caused by Carlino and the twins would recommence, reinforced by the baby's cries, broken by Teresina's supplications and Signora Soave's moans.

This routine was repeated every day.

November passed. Gray fog was followed by snow, a thick snow falling unbroken on the street, covering the grass and stones, deadening the footsteps of the rare passerby. The white snow weighing on the rooftops made glaring reflections. The eternal, continual snow descended slowly, so thickly it sometimes looked like a curtain in front of the window.

Then the Caccias' parlor became even darker. Teresina had to stand on the wooden step with the curtains raised, her forehead against the window, sewing hurriedly in the brief hours of daylight. From time to time she raised her tired eyes to look at the street, the Varisi mansion, hermetically sealed, all dark in the middle of the snow.

"Put your work down. Move around a little," her mother said.

Where? Outside of the parlor, the house was freezing. Teresina suffered from the cold and the skin on her hands was cracked. She preferred to stay in her somber niche working and looking at the snow.

The inner voice of youth no longer spoke to her tranquil spirit. Teresina was calm and chaste. A faint sensation rising in her breast, at certain moments a languor in her eyes, betrayed the ferment unconsciously forming. Then she looked more intensely at the white veil before her, the high walls and the sky. Through prolonged and distracted concentration she glimpsed a distant, blurred horizon.

December came with its festivities, with gay activities in the house, with solemn religious services. December, the children's month, when the twins received a new doll that Carlino broke immediately under the pretext of improving it. And in December little Ida, the smallest, got her first tooth.

January swept away the snow. The sun shone, but it was colder than ever. Signor Caccia warned them they had to cut back on the use of firewood if it was to last all winter.

In the Portalupis' house there was unusual activity. The three young women went to the balls held at the Areses' house every two weeks. The little dressmaker ran back and forth with boxes to fit and refit, while the head dressmaker from Cremona made certain mysterious expeditions in great haste and sent packages of samples.

On the evenings of the dance, Teresina would stand at the window to watch the large carriage leave, and looking closely at the windows would see the whiteness of veils today, a bluish reflection tomorrow. Now the glitter of a jewel, another time a softly provocative pink leather glove—and the heavy carriage would pass noisily with the clip-clop of the two good Romagna horses, leaving in Teresa's eyes the dazzling brilliance of a vision.

"That's quite a show, isn't it?" said the judge's wife one evening—she had a loose tongue. Like a good neighbor she came, kerchief on her head, every six or seven days on the evenings her little urchins went to sleep early. She added: "They really want to get their three ugly girls married."

"It's the second one they talk about, I think," Signora Soave countered.

"For the subprefect? But they tried to pass the first one off on him. In my opinion no one wants her. You can't trust these Southerners! I lived down there four years, and I know them."

"They have a nice dowry."

"At least that's what they say. However, we, dear Signora, weren't married for our dowries, were we?"

Signora Soave pulled her shawl across her chest, almost as

though to hide the regret she alone knew, and replied: "One does what one can."

"Certainly, I understand, when there are daughters to get married . . . thank goodness mine are still young. But not yours. You have a grown girl already."

She looked at Teresina, who was beet red, feeling suddenly ashamed.

"Teresina is still young."

"Yes, but if a good match should come along? . . ."

"It's all destiny," Signora Soave interrupted gravely with that woeful inflection in her voice that accompanied the dullness in her dark eyes.

Then February came and March.

Spring brought no change in the family's monotonous routine, except that windows were opened and rays of new light, the sound of footsteps, the murmur of voices entered from the street.

Windows in other houses also opened, revealing freshly starched muslin curtains. Pots of flowers kept inside from the cold reappeared on windowsills, dry geraniums, dusty verbena. Only the little green and luxuriant wallflowers had sprouted their first buds.

At old Tisbe's window, winter shawls, hand-knitted petticoats, flannel vests danced in the wind.

Giovanni Boccabadati's house was more shut than ever. One morning he left elegantly dressed, carrying a little traveling bag of Russian leather with lock and nielloed decoration. His old servant, mute as a sphinx, accompanied him to the door. Then the door closed again hermetically, as if the old man were entombing himself.

"Don Giovanni's after money," the judge's wife said on that occasion. "He takes flight like the swallows . . ."

Teresina thought awhile about what the judge's wife had said. She thought it would be nice to fly like Don Giovanni on a nice April morning, with a little traveling bag, fly away through the world into the unknown, fly through green and flowering country, over blue lakes, over fantastic mountains, through enchanting cities; or fly like the little swallows in her garden to their sweet little nests barely large enough for two.

Teresina looked tenderly at those nests attached to the portico rafters, happy with young loves, celebrating new broods. Only one nest remained empty in the sadness of widowhood, in the irremediable sadness of bygone days.

Beyond the portico extended a piece of land, with some exaggeration called a garden. In truth, it had some flower beds that at first sight confirmed the illusion, particularly at that time of year, since the pansies were in bloom with their infinite shades, with the intense velvet of their dark leaves and the luminous silk of their pale leaves; and above them trembled two flowering bushes like a snow bank.

A few yards beyond began an attempt at a kitchen garden and orchard containing a rudimentary row of lettuce amid masses of sage, rosemary, and fennel, in the company of a slender peach tree sparsely dotted with little pink flowers.

Beyond that nothing. The gravelly soil, full of lime, refused to grow anything. Only a fig tree in the corner, tree of sterile lands, raised its knotty branches above the garden wall.

Chapter V

How had her father's old aunt ever forced herself to leave Marcaria,* where she had been born sixty years ago, and where she had spent her entire honest, obscure life?

Teresina was amazed by, but above all happy about, the affection the good old woman showed her. She was happy beyond belief because now she had promised to go back to Marcaria with her for a two-week visit.

At first Signor Caccia had said no, shaking his head, arching his eyebrows in such a way that Teresina didn't dare breathe. It had been Signora Soave, with unusual courage, with tears in her eyes as always, to plead with her husband, to convince him that a little innocent distraction would be good for the girl.

"Mamma, what will you do?" Teresina said, because she felt it her duty to say it.

"Don't worry, Teresa. It's only a few days."

"And if the baby isn't good?"

"She'll be good. Go."

"And if the twins won't let you comb their hair?"

"They will. Don't worry. And enjoy your vacation in peace as long as you can! . . ."

Signora Soave said these last words so sadly, as if she knew her

* A village to the west of the Oglio River in the province of Mantua.

days of pleasure were numbered, that her daughter hugged and kissed her.

Aunt Rosa, in the serenity of her placid life, had kept a little of the statuesque beauty that at eighteen had thrown her into the arms of a man without either of them loving the other, because he needed a wife to help with his shop, and she was of marriageable age.

From then on she, calm and faithful, had kept the shop, apparently ignoring the numerous absences of her husband, who was involved in an old relationship that often kept him away from home. She had had sixteen or seventeen children, but had never known love, never been loved. Continually nursing or pregnant, she was absorbed in these cares and, beguiled or satisfied by the appearance of love, she didn't feel the lack of it. And so, after raising so many children, she found herself alone, with white hair, because almost all were dead, and the few living had sought their fortune far away. She had remained alone behind the counter, always calm, with her pretty statuary arms resting on her apron, until her husband's infirmities required her presence and she had to give up the shop.

Now she was taking Teresina back with her, and the passive goodness of the woman was gratified by the girl's joy, like a placid return to her own youth, to the youth she had lost without rapture or without regret. She quietly observed the chasteness of her smile and deportment, her unconscious charm, until she was moved to tenderness.

Barely sixteen years old!

Signora Soave, with her babe in arms, walked them to the carriage waiting in the street.

"Good-bye, Mamma. I'll be back soon."

"Yes. Don't worry about us."

"Ida's white dress is in the top drawer of my dresser, if you need it."

"Yes, yes."

"I'll write you, Mamma."

Signora Soave was unable to reply. Leaning against the door frame, she shielded her eyes from the sun, but behind her hands her eyes were shining.

"How much your mamma loves you!" whispered Aunt Rosa.

"Oh, yes, yes, she loves me," Teresina confirmed jubilantly, taking her place in the carriage as happy as if she were stepping up to a throne. And in that overwhelming elation, she looked up to see old Tisbe at her window and saluted her with an exaggerated bow.

To tease her, Carlino whispered in her ear: "You look just like the oldest Portalupi daughter when she greets the subprefect."

Teresina laughed.

At the first undulations of the carriage as the horses started up, Teresina felt her heart pounding, as if her whole life were on the verge of changing. She blew another kiss to her mamma, glancing sideways at the judge's door in case there was someone there to see her, and she was disappointed that all the Portalupis' windows were closed.

However, crossing the town was a triumph. Luzzi, who was smoking a cigar at the café, raised his hat with such a flourish she blushed. Next to him Don Giovanni Boccabadati, indolent and distracted, also looked at her through half-closed eyes. The pharmacist came to the doorway and craned his neck to see. Near the church two women, the mayor's wife and Doctor Tavecchia's sister, smiled kindly.

All told, Teresina had bowed her head many times and had held herself so straight that the moment they entered the main road outside the town, she let go with a great sigh of relief and leaned back on the leather cushions.

Accustomed to continual activity, she enjoyed these moments

of idleness. She felt like a great lady and looked around with pleasure, observing the trees and road and sky as though seeing them for the first time.

Not in the least fanciful, she was nevertheless elated by being transported through dust clouds down a long, long road. She imagined all the dust was raised for her, the horse ran for her, and the happy squeak of the rickety carriage springs was for her—for her and her aunt.

She felt infinite gratitude toward God, an impulse of love for nature and her fellow creatures. How beautiful everything in the world was! How good everyone was!

The little villages, the little cottages scattered through the countryside, excited her interest. Certainly peaceful families lived there, loving fathers and mothers and happy children.

What wonderful races alongside the hedgerows! What happy singing in the meadows in the evenings, with fireflies glowing! Now everything was splendid. Everything sparkled in the sunshine. The smooth, yellow, winding road was lost in the intense green grasses of the country. Throughout the plain there was only green, the uniform green of the first hay crop, the various greens of oak and walnut trees, the pale green of willow trees, and high above it all, silhouetted against the sky, the rustling poplar trees.

"Aunty, is it much further?"

"A little!"

She was thinking how happy Carlino would have been in her place, and in the uncorrupted goodness of her heart she almost regretted her joy; but then she consoled herself by promising to take a weaned nightingale to her brother, something he so badly wanted.

"There are nightingales in Marcaria, aren't there?"

"Are there? I believe so . . . certainly, certainly, there must be."

Aunt Rosa responded calmly, keeping her hands crossed over her ample matron's breast to restrain her mantilla fluttering in the breeze.

Teresina eagerly drank in that breeze, leaning out of the carriage, unconcerned about sun and dust, content to blink her eyes when she could no longer see.

"Is it much further, Aunty?"

"A bit!"

A sulky, pulled by a black horse, came up like a flash.

"Can anyone be more mad than that?" exclaimed her aunt, methodically fastening her mantilla with a pin she had found.

At that point the road became narrower. Running at breakneck speed, the sulky hit a wheel of their carriage, breaking one of the spokes.

The driver immediately stopped the carriage with a curse and stepped down to examine the damage, while her Aunt Rosa, calm and smiling, urged Teresina not to be afraid.

"It's nothing," said the driver, "but it could have been worse."

The sulky had also stopped. The driver, a dark young man, courteously came to inquire if the women had been frightened. They were not.

Then the young man gave something to the driver to pay for the wheel. He climbed back on the sulky and, lightly touching his cap, left at a trot.

"Thoughtless young people!" concluded Aunt Rosa.

"That one is more thoughtless than all the rest," replied the driver.

"Do you know him?"

"How could I not know him? You meet him everywhere. Here today, tomorrow at Mantova. Mornings dashing through the countryside in the sulky, evenings at Parma or Cremona. That's Orlandi."

"Oh, Orlandi? exclaimed Teresina. "If I had known it was Orlandi I'd have taken a better look."

She stuck her head outside the carriage, but already far away, the sulky appeared no more than a black dot in the dust.

"They talked about him a lot last year during the flood," replied Teresina, regretting she hadn't looked at him.

The scorching noonday sun descended on the countryside. Over the green plains a soft incandescent layer of sun and dust spread like melted gold, heavy and solemn under a milky, uniform sky. No bird's cry, no rustling wing, no song broke the high midday silence—the silence of deserted fields, of nature in repose, of mute and mysterious woods.

Teresina renewed her question: "Is it much further?"

And this time her aunt answered: "Just a little bit."

When they lowered the drawbridge at Marcaria and the carriage passed the Oglio over that rusty contraption, Teresina had trouble containing her amazement. Her brother Carlino really should be there.

As far as she was concerned, she had a very incomplete and vague notion about drawbridges, and her restricted imagination didn't suggest medieval phantasms. Nevertheless, it looked like an extraordinary thing, worthy of being remembered when she told them about her trip at home.

Her uncle was waiting for her, immobilized in his armchair, with his legs propped on a straw stool. He was a large, robust old man with thick wiry hair, shifty eyes, and a sensual mouth. He looked his niece over with the rapid, sure glance of an ancient womanizer.

His wife was solicitous, asking him how he got along and if his leg was better. He made a few grumbling noises, lowering his head while he tapped his knee.

Impulsively, Teresina threw her arms around his neck and felt her uncle's cold lips as she gave him a kiss. She immediately drew back, but he emitted a soft shout of pleasure, looking at her with shining eyes thanking her, until pain brought his hands back to his knees, his head collapsed on his chest.

"Was it right to bring her back?" Aunt Rosa asked him softly.

He nodded yes.

"Prospero is well, and so are his wife and children. They told me to give you their greetings."

Again the nod of his head.

"This poor little girl hasn't seen a thing. She lives the life of an old woman in her house. You know how Prospero is."

The old man suddenly raised his head. "How old is she?"

"Just turned sixteen."

The word "sixteen" stopped in the air, as though suspended over the heads of the couple, who were looking at each other, struck by the same thought.

Aunt Rosa sighed calmly, with her hands relaxed on her lap. Her husband made an angry grimace and went back to rubbing his knees, his eyes staring ahead, his lips pursed.

Meanwhile Teresina had run to the door that led to the garden. It was a splash of light, of green, of flowering roses. A beautiful hound dog slept in the sun, two little kittens played with a bobbin. Teresina smiled at the sun, at the flowers, at her own youth, which glowed on every surrounding object. She felt strong, she had an appetite, her legs tingled with exuberant life, her pulse hammered pleasantly with a gay refrain full of promises.

When her aunt called her, she skipped like a deer, defying the gravity of the trailing skirt she was wearing for the first time, so completely happy that if they had told her to fly she would have tried it at once.

"Are you bored?" asked Aunt Rosa in an old mamma's kindly tone. "This house is a little gloomy for a young person."

"No, no, oh, no," Teresina protested sincerely, tasting the joy (new to her) of absolute lack of responsibility. She looked around the large empty room curiously. It was a little cold, a little mildewed, where the two old people seemed to have outlived so many of their memories.

"This is the counter," the aunt said pointing to the large, dark oak piece. "The store counter."

"Oh, yes?"

"On this divan Giovanni, my next to last son, was sick for seven months."

"Poor boy!"

"That picture, do you see, that embroidered picture, the Madonna of Sorrows? It was the work of my poor Giudittina for her exams the last year of boarding school."

"Beautiful!"

"Look at the hands. She worked two and a half months just on the hands."

"Ooh! Really?"

Teresina remained ecstatic and sweetly touched by all those memories until her uncle, propping himself on the arms of the chair, made a move to rise.

"It's time to eat. The clock's struck one, and the girl must be hungry."

Then a peculiar look flashed across his face and he muttered through his toothless mouth, "Sixteen years old!"

Chapter VI

Waking up in a new room the next morning brought new pleasures.

First Teresa had awakened with a start, thinking she heard the twins crying and quarreling with each other, but she smiled when she realized her mistake. Drawing back the leg she already had outside the bed, she cuddled up comfortably under the sheet. The soft mattress over a sack of feathers gave under her body, forming a warm little niche into which the delighted girl sank. She lay on her side with her hands on her chest, knees slightly bent, head abandoned on the thin pillow, and she looked around.

There was nothing special about that room, but for Teresina everything was new, from the bed to the beautiful earthenware basin with blue flowers. Four modest little pictures on the wall represented the adventures of Telemachus; Venus, leading Love to the island of Calypso, was painted in a pink dress with puffed sleeves. Teresina did not wonder if that attire corresponded with classical tradition. She saw only a beautiful woman dressed in pink amid so many others dressed in white, with young Telemachus among them. There was nothing objectionable about the scene to her mind.

Facing her bed at home was Santa Lucia with her eyes on a platter. The comparison was all to the advantage of Telemachus's adventures.

A faint rustling at the door made her call out. Aunt Rosa came in, peaceful and calm with a demitasse of coffee in her hand.

The shame of being surprised in bed made Teresina babble a great number of excuses, but her aunt smilingly cut them off by saying that when she was Teresina's age, she loved to sleep, and that Teresina must be a little tired after the trip yesterday.

"But you're already up . . ."

"Oh! that's different. I got out of the habit of sleeping when I nursed my babies, and then someone was always sick. Now I'm old. I don't sleep much anymore."

She said "I don't sleep much anymore" calmly, with her inveterate lethargy, as if her life, day or night, responded only to the simple mechanism of material functions.

Teresina didn't want to take the coffee. She wasn't accustomed to it. Only Mamma drank coffee in her house.

"That doesn't matter. You're not at home now," added Aunt Rosa with her good encouraging smile.

And when Teresina drank it obediently, she felt a light lashing of her nerves, a complete sense of well-being, an unusual energy, a strange mental lucidity. Her aunt left the room. She picked up the cup she had put on the little table and drank the last drop happily, licking her lips. Then she leaped out of bed like a spring.

No one made her anxious. Her mamma didn't call, "Teresina, Teresina," with that small tired voice she knew so well. No twins' hair to comb. No breakfast to prepare. None of Ida's diapers to carefully roll. Not her father's gruff voice: "Don't anyone touch the papers in my study!"

A whole room to herself—an unconfined area, absolute freedom.

She began to dress slowly, tasting the pleasure of walking barefooted on the rug between the bed and wall and whirling in her skirt without a corset, periodically pulling up the blouse that would slip to her arms.

How white her arms were! She had never had time to look at

them before. They looked like someone else's arms, slender, round, white. She couldn't make out why they were white while her face and even her neck were darker. Only under her collar bone, where her breasts began, did the white reappear.

This unevenness of her skin color surprised her. It couldn't be natural. Then she was suddenly struck by a strange thought. Was she pretty or ugly?

If only she were pretty!

She went up to the mirror to examine herself in detail, up so close she could see her breath on it. She carefully cleaned it off, first with her hand and then with a napkin until it was shining, and looked again at her reflection. But the doubt was still there.

As she looked at herself, she didn't feel the awe beauty arouses. Just the opposite. With some discomfort she realized her nose was not straight like Aunt Rosa's, who had been a real beauty; and even her cheeks and chin did not have those pure lines that made her aunt look like a marble statue.

Was she, therefore, ugly? Teresina was about to reach that conclusion when she gave one last general survey that embraced the entire harmony of her face, which gave her a good impression, and she felt consoled. She didn't seem beautiful, but neither was she ugly like the Portalupis.

For a moment she searched for a word, a word applicable to her own features, but one didn't come to her right away.

Then she decided to get dressed, and did it with unusual care: tightening her corset, making sure her hair was parted exactly in the middle.

"I'm beginning to get some self-*esteem!*" she said, smiling to herself in the mirror at the funny idea that she could *esteem* herself. She stood stock still, struck by the sparkle she saw on her full red lips and dazzling white teeth. She smiled again. How odd! Her whole face changed. Was that the effect she made when she laughed?

And she felt overcome by a curious happiness; she continued to laugh and jump around the room, wanting to sing, dance, embrace someone.

Suddenly she stopped, giving herself a little shake.

Going into the courtyard to take the air like a serious, composed young lady, she looked kindly at the snoozing hound stretched out in his pen. She walked about in the garden, bending to smell the roses carefully, like an expert.

"Pick some roses," her uncle shouted from behind her.

The old man had been watching her from the breakfast room window, his thin hands resting on the windowsill.

Teresina chose a few roses, leaving the unopened buds alone, preferring those full blown. Taking them from her apron she smelled each one before gathering them into a bouquet, and then smelled them again with her face deep in the fresh petals, bathing her cheeks in dew.

"They're beautiful, aren't they?"

"Very beautiful."

Teresina continued to walk slowly, looking for more roses among the bushes, holding to her chest those roses escaping from her fingers.

"Let me see."

Teresina went up to the window where the old man was now struggling to remain upright and showed him the roses, brushing his ice-cold hands.

He smelled them a moment and then staggered and fell into the armchair with his head lolling on his chest. The frightened girl dropped the roses on the windowsill and ran to look for her aunt.

"A little weakness, that's all," her aunt said, holding an expert hand on her husband's head.

After a warm broth he recovered, and when a little glass of

Malaga was added to the broth, the old man's eyes began to sparkle, then they concentrated greedily on the scattered roses.

In half an hour he was asleep.

"Men are much weaker than we are," Aunt Rosa said quietly as she knitted a wool stocking.

"Yes?" asked Teresina, incredulous.

"Yes."

Her aunt added no more. Those words came from long, singular, sure experience. In that assertion synthesizing the weakness of the strong sex was the fruit of a lifetime spent quietly watching from behind the shop counter and at the bedsides of her sixteen children throughout the slow, patient hours of female solitude.

Teresina wasn't able to understand, and she didn't understand, but she was impressed by a serious thought as she watched those two old people: one decrepit, angrily attached to life; the other serenely matter of fact—beautiful in the marmoreal calm of her body, which no breath of passion had ever altered. Her uncle frightened her a little, and secretly aroused a certain repugnance. However, she never tired of watching Aunt Rosa, sitting with the majesty of an ancient Roman matron, methodically working the knitting needles with her plump hands, occasionally raising her crystal-clear eyes.

She wrote her mother, "Aunt Rosa is as good as she is beautiful."

Who in the world was the tall, thin young man in cinnamon-colored trousers who passed under her window this morning just as she was closing the shutters?

She found out one day at the table as her aunt dished out the thin noodles: "I don't know what's wrong with Cecchino, the postmaster's son. He goes by here five or six times a day."

She learned his name, and she learned he was the son of a postal employee. Observing him closer, she also realized he was not ugly, but a little sickly looking, with large protruding eyes that tried to grasp people like a pair of pliers.

It was entertaining to watch him pass by every morning, and he was useful for telling the time: Cecchino meant exactly seven-thirty.

Aunt Rosa, who knew the postmaster's family, didn't say no one evening when they came to ask if Teresina could go dance a few rounds to accordion music. And Teresina, who had never danced in her life, felt her heart take a dive. Certainly, she was happy, but she had so little self-assurance and such a fear of appearing awkward and unskilled that she preferred to keep out of sight.

As she entered the room with all the chairs lined up along the walls, the floor sprinkled with fresh water, and four candles attached to four little mirrors, she felt a moment of dizziness. She saw no one and looked at nothing. Like a sleepwalker she went to the darkest corner, where there was a humble, forgotten little chair in the window space hung with a white blanket disguised as a drape.

Teresina sat down and stayed there as though glued to the seat.

She dumbly watched two or three couples whirling around, and from the other side of the room Aunt Rosa appeared to be gesturing for her to come out of that corner, to do like the others. But there was a fog before her eyes that kept her from seeing her surroundings clearly. And the fog expanded until it became a murky darkness, after which something cinnamon colored stopped in front of her.

"May I?"

What was she supposed to do? What was being offered? Who was speaking? Energetically she replied, No, no, pushing away a paper bag.

"Please, take one, it's only candy."

Was it really? Wasn't it a joke? Weren't they little rocks or bits of bread? Her brother had played that trick on her many times.

The voice kept insisting, and Teresina decided to reach out and take a piece.

"You don't dance?"

Little by little Teresina recovered from her daze, and her eyes began to see more clearly. Signor Cecchino had a nice voice. He stood there so respectfully she had the deep desire to please him by accepting his courtesies.

She replied sweetly: "I've never danced."

"You don't know how to dance?"

"Oh, at school . . . or with my little sisters . . ."

"It's the same thing. Take a turn with me. I'm sure you dance divinely."

He put the candy in a jacket pocket and took her hand gallantly.

"I'm afraid my head will spin . . ."

"Nothing to fear. I have a strong arm, you won't fall with me."

To give her speedy proof of his strength, he encircled her narrow waist.

Teresina fell again into darkness. She was no longer conscious of herself, turning, turning, blinded by the four candles like dazzling pinwheels, feeling the paper bag of candy that Cecchino had in his pocket against her hip, not daring to tell him not to hold her so tightly.

"Are you tired?"

She was dying, but didn't have the courage to admit it. She was intoxicated by the movement, the leaping music, the warmth of that body next to hers, the strong smell of jasmine emanating from her partner's hair.

"You dance like an angel."

Fortunately the accordion stopped playing. Teresina fell on the first chair, her face red as a glowing ember.

The second, third time she danced with Cecchino she was less fearful, but her excitement had increased. By the end of the evening she had reached such a state she was unable to speak without her voice trembling; and when he said, drawling his words and making his eyes expressive: "I'm so sorry the time has passed so quickly!" she, beside herself in rapture, asked: "Why?"

Cecchino wasted no time in answering: "Because I have to leave someone so nice."

The room reeled like a spindle, the accordion and its player reeled, Aunt Rosa reeled, Teresa reeled clasped in Cecchino's arms.

It was really only those two spinning around, at the final beat of the last dance.

"Did you enjoy yourself?" Aunt Rosa asked when they were home.

"Very much," replied Teresina with a conviction that showed in her eyes.

Once in her room, she happily went over in her mind every phrase of that memorable dance, remembering word for word everything Cecchino had said: "May I? Please, take one, it's only candy. You aren't dancing?" everything, everything up to the words "someone so nice." Just thinking about them made her heart pound.

She looked lovingly at the piece of candy, torn between the desire to eat it and to keep it forever.

The bed felt hard, the covers too heavy. She was tired but couldn't close her eyes. As soon as her eyes felt heavy she would jump, seeming to hear "someone so nice" coming from her pillow. And then she remembered the accordion refrains and hugged the mattress with her left arm held high, her right arm stretched out in the illusion of dancing again. At dawn she slept.

On awaking her first thought was of him, but instead of being a gay and happy thought it came almost like pain, like a sharp thorn in her skin.

As the day passed her melancholy grew. She had never felt such sadness. She felt different, as if a great number of years were weighing on her, along with sad thoughts of death, illness, discomfort, emptiness.

She touched her dress here and there where he had touched it, and was overcome by a great desire to weep.

At the dinner hour, her heart was so oppressed she couldn't swallow her food.

"Go lie down, poor thing, you're tired."

Teresina didn't make her say it twice. It hurt to keep such restraint in the company of her aunt and uncle. She felt the need for solitude, to be alone with the new person lodging in her, to be able to close her eyes and think of Signor Cecchino.

The second night was no better, nor the following day. In the morning she saw him pass by the window, and the long look he gave her made her happy for a moment, but then persistent, painful melancholy took over.

"This girl is sick," Aunt Rosa said, caressing her sweetly. "Maybe the air is bad for you."

"No, Aunty, it's not making me sick."

"You are restless and pale. Let me feel your pulse. Does your head hurt?"

"A little."

"Leave her alone," the old man interfered, casting sideways one of his penetrating looks. "It's nothing."

"I believe it's nothing, but now and then young people need some tonic. When my children didn't feel good I'd give them a spoonful of manna. Do you want a spoonful of manna, Teresina? It's sweet."

And because Teresina was pacing the room at a little distance, the old man cupped his hands around his mouth in the direction of his wife: "She's in love!"

And he sneered, shaking his head at the ignorance of the good woman. She couldn't say a thing, staring straight ahead with those crystal-clear eyes that had seen many things in life, but never love.

Chapter VII

Signor Caccia came unexpectedly to get his daughter. She didn't even try to argue, although she had trouble holding back her tears.

"She's too sensitive," Signora Rosa said. "Just like her mother, blessed woman."

When her uncle told her good-bye, he whispered: "Cheer up, everything passes. Look, this is the only ill without a cure," and he pointed to his bad leg and white hair.

Teresina gave him a little smile. In the depths of her sorrow she still felt her youth, and illusions sang higher and stronger than all brief human experience.

Before she left she saw him, waiting in front of the post office as her carriage went by. They exchanged a passionate look, and for the whole trip Teresina thought of nothing but that look.

The road seemed very long and sad, but when she saw the first houses of her little town thoughts of her mamma and sisters absorbed her almost completely.

As they passed through the piazza, she looked around excitedly. The buildings were all familiar—the pharmacy, the café, the town hall. As usual the hatter had his felt forms spread out on benches to dry. The milliner, that lazy woman, was gawking from the doorway of her shop.

Everything was as before, only Teresina had changed. The things she saw were the same, but she saw them differently.

Signora Soave immediately noticed the difference in her daughter. "How you've grown up," she told her.

Then they had a long chat. The little one had been a nuisance; she never slept at night. The capricious twins gave her no peace; they tore up everything. Their elbows were already out of their red and black striped dresses—were there pieces to patch them? Teresina assured her there were.

At least Carlino was good. You could live with him if you let him turn his room upside down, set traps for mice, play with sap covered sticks, break a chair, and go out occasionally for a good time with his chums.

Teresina listened docilely while Signora Soave chattered on. As the children were at school and Ida was in bed, she had a minute to rest. She sat on the divan with a stool under her feet, a gray shawl crossed over her breast, each little yellow hand decorated with horsehair bracelets.

"And did you have a good time?"

"Yes, Mamma."

"Your aunt and uncle were nice to you?"

"Very nice. Especially Aunt Rosa. She never got mad and never complained about anything. She's happy, don't you think?"

"Who is ever happy in this world! . . . Teresina, you don't know yet. No, you don't know."

Signora Soave's black eyes rolled dejectedly to heaven. Teresina had the crazy impulse to reveal her secret, but she didn't dare right at that moment.

After a little, without any preamble, as if an unknown power drew out the words, she exclaimed, "I danced."

"You danced? At Marcaria? Not in your uncle's house, I suppose."

"No, in the postmaster's house."

"Who was there?"

"The doctor and his wife, the host's son, two Cacciamali girls . . ."

It was a good opportunity. Cecchino's name burned on the girl's lips. She had only mentioned the dance in order to talk about him; she wanted to tell her mother everything. But that name wouldn't come out. Two or three attempts were aborted. An inexplicable knot squeezed her throat, and her heart beat crazily.

"Your father's in a bad mood. Didn't you notice? Business isn't going well."

What business? Teresina didn't know anything about it. She only knew the opportunity to say something had passed.

The twins and Carlino came home together. "Did you bring me a nightingale?"

Teresina had to confess she had forgotten, and blamed herself to high heaven for her absentmindedness. The little girls threw themselves on her, asking if she had brought them something from Marcaria.

"Just what should I have brought you?"

She was rather annoyed; for the first time she felt cross with her sisters.

However, the twins were not discouraged. They attached themselves to either side of her skirt, caressing her, rummaging around until they found a piece of candy in her pocket. Then pandemonium broke out.

"Give me my candy," Teresina shouted in exasperation.

Not a chance. The twins defended their find with their fists.

"I want my candy," Teresina replied with tears in her eyes, preparing to take it by force.

Signora Soave, who at first thought Teresina was joking, and then realized she was angry, was obliged to scold her gently. How could she make the little girls cry over a piece of candy?

Her daughter realized the justice of the scolding and a bright flame of shame rose to her cheeks. She said no more, allowing the candy to be shared equally between the twins, while she smothered her sobs with her apron to her face.

"A message, a message!" the girls cried.

"It's a talking sweet," Carlino said.

Teresina looked over her apron, and seeing Carlino grab for the paper, blurted: "At least give me that."

"I'll read it first."

"No, it's mine."

"Not anymore."

"Yes."

"No."

Teresina was overcome by anger, spite, desolation at losing the only souvenir of the dance left to her.

Carlino read aloud, declaiming mockingly: "Remember, tyrant with a cruel heart, your faithful lover who dies for you."

With a breaking heart, Teresina brusquely put out her hand. With equal agility, Carlino retracted his. The paper tore in half.

Incapable of further self-control, the girl ran to shut herself in her room, where she completely broke down.

All summer long she rocked herself in thoughts of that love, nourishing extravagant illusions. Sometimes she imagined Signor Cecchino was passing by on Via di San Francesco, or going around the suburbs incognito, waiting for the opportunity to see her. Perhaps she would receive a letter. Perhaps he was disposed to come ask her to marry him.

All these fantasies kept her very busy changing the sequence of her ideas.

About this time, she began reading romances under the indulgent eyes of her mother.

"It's not at all true, you know," Signora Soave said languidly.

"Life isn't like it's described in books. But I read them, too, at your age. Things of youth."

Once when a letter arrived from her uncle in Marcaria, Teresina thought she would lose her mind. The letter had been put on the tax collector's table in his study, and she walked around it impatiently, looking at it, touching it, trying to see if there was something discreetly transparent about the envelope.

When Signor Caccia put on his glasses, ripped open the seal and read the few words in the blink of an eye and put the letter in his pocket, Teresina remained open mouthed, with her heart in suspense. As Signor Caccia walked away she found the courage to run after him. "Doesn't it say anything?"

The authoritarian "what?" of her father and his dreadfully frowning eyebrows made her retreat, adding in confusion, and trembling because of the falsehood: "Is there a greeting for me . . . from Aunt Rosa?"

Often when she had put the twins to bed and said her prayers, about to go to bed herself, she would sit half dressed on the edge of her bed thinking of that evening.

If an organ grinder passed while she was sewing below on the wooden step by the window, the music would send shivers down her back with memories of delicious sensations.

On hot July afternoons during the promenade along the river bank, and later in the piazza where the young men of the town lazed around, she could imagine the secret of those comings and goings, the pauses, the broken-off sentences, the mysterious gestures. There was Luzzi, Boccabadati, the carabinieri lieutenant, the pharmacist; sometimes Orlandi, two or three others, and in the middle of them all, Teresina would search eagerly and in vain.

In November during the fair, the theater opened with a fairly good company of singers performing *Rigoletto*.

Carlino, who had gone once (with tickets for the gallery that cost eighty centesimi), could sing the opera's main arias. His sister listened to him, repeating them in a low voice, remembering all the words. She liked the duke's declaration of love to Maddalena, but most of all she liked Gilda's aria, "Tutte le feste al tempio."

She wanted Carlino to explain who Rigoletto was, and who was the young man his daughter met at the temple.

Carlino gave some sketchy, approximate details; he described Sparafucile's awful face and the ridiculous hunchback of the court jester.

"But Gilda, Gilda?"

He shrugged. "Gilda mewed like a cat. And besides, you know I don't watch the women."

Teresina, who had never flattered herself she would ever go to the theater, was happier than she had been for some time the day the judge's wife came to tell her mother: "I have a key to box seats this evening. My sister-in-law and I are going. Will you let Teresina go with us?

Signora Soave delicately made the observation that it would be too crowded with three women.

The judge's wife insisted, but it was necessary to persuade Signor Caccia, because nothing could be done without his consent. Among the arguments of the judge's wife was this: Teresina was now grown and if they wanted her to marry they had to let her be seen.

Signor Caccia consented grumpily. A few little difficulties arose regarding her hairstyle. And Signora Soave felt Teresina didn't have a suitable dress, but the judge's wife solved this problem also, assuring her that when a girl has her hair fixed nicely, with a pair of clean gloves and a flower, she can go anywhere.

As long as everything was undecided Teresina was on pins and needles; when finally every obstacle was removed, and she was certain about the enjoyment awaiting her, she allowed herself to feel happy.

She hugged her mother and the judge's wife; she ran up and down the stairs three or four times without any purpose; she went to the window, opened drawers, began working on something, stopped.

"That girl's getting big ideas," Signor Caccia pronounced. "Troubles are just beginning."

"But it's her age, Prospero. We were young once."

Signora Soave lovingly watched her daughter leave, just as when she left for Marcaria, following her with damp eyes full of tenderness and hope.

The judge's wife, an easygoing woman, suggested Teresina adopt a relaxed manner. Remembering her first introduction to society, Teresina assured her she was no longer a novice. In fact, she felt a certain boldness. However, once seated in the box it was entirely different, when she looked around and saw the triple row of lights, and all those heads below, and so many others above her. She felt everyone was looking at her.

"Well, Teresina, you're like a statue. Say something."

The sister-in-law thought it would be better to let her get used to things gradually. Then the two women began talking at the back of the box. In front of them, leaning on the railing, Teresina watched the crowd, recognizing faces here and there.

The three Portalupi sisters were in the second row, dressed in bright yellow with three bright yellow fans. In the neighboring box the subprefect, very distinguished and elegant with his handsome beard parted southern-style, his cuffs shining like porcelain, and his impertinent myopic eyes taking in all the women nearby.

The entire Arese family, the women in velvet dresses and diamonds; the men serious, solemn, a slight boredom painted on their faces.

The mayor's wife in black (the same dress she wore to Mass), having come out of a sense of obligation, without understanding a thing, hoping the performance would soon end.

In the first row of boxes, Don Giovanni, alone, stretched out on two chairs, yawning.

"Who is that gentleman?" asked the sister-in-law, who was new to town.

The judge's wife replied in a lower voice: "He's Boccabadati, cock of the walk."

"He doesn't look like one."

"Really, here he does! He knows all the women. They say he comes for the contralto, the one who plays Maddalena."

"Is he rich?"

"Rich enough, but the women don't leave him much." She lowered her voice a tone. "See that tall, pale woman there in the stalls?"

"Wearing a veil? And a red rose?"

"That's the one. She's the milliner on the piazza. A few years ago he had . . ." a pause . . . "and he had to fork over a goodly sum."

"Really?"

"For her son."

Teresina listened, back straight, immobile. She couldn't see the milliner, who had her back to her, but Don Giovanni was in front of her in all his sybaritic indifference, plump, florid, already pervaded by the languor that awaits men in their forties who have enjoyed life on a vast scale. After what she had heard, that great self-satisfaction bothered her. She was deeply vexed by a mystery that continually evaded her.

In another moment, her attention was entirely absorbed by the spectacle. She didn't blink or breathe. As soon as a character's mouth opened, she was all ears. Her eyes carefully followed every movement. After the curtain fell, she turned suddenly to the judge's wife.

"And Gilda?"

"Gilda will come next, in the second act."

"That court jester seems evil."

"No, he's not evil, you'll see."

"And the duke?"

"Ah, the duke . . . you'll see, you'll see."

Gilda appeared dressed in white, not pretty, but rather young, and with a modest air that immediately appealed to Teresina. She sang well, with more feeling than voice, flavoring the tale of her love of the student with a subtle melancholy.

Teresina was enraptured. The beauty of art revealed itself to her heart already open to love. She anxiously followed the development of the dramatic action. The kidnapping of Gilda frightened her, she cried with Rigoletto, she had disrespect and scorn for the courtesans, and waited excitedly for Gilda's return to the stage.

At this point, a fog of incomprehension fell over her thoughts again. She was tempted to ask why Gilda was so desperate at finding herself in the duke's house. A vague instinct suggested her question was ridiculous, and she remained quiet, pondering.

She burned with anger at the duke in the forest scene. Maddalena seemed coarse, incapable of arousing love. Gilda's tragic end with the cynical duke in the background softly singing struck her deeply. She had to shrink back in the darkness to hide her tears.

"What are you doing, child. Are you so easily affected? It's not true, you know. Gilda will soon go to supper full of good feelings for her lover."

In this way the judge's wife tried to calm Teresina, but not succeeding because she was unaware of the source of her emotions. The intense passion of that story of love found a secret and intimate correspondence in the soul of the young girl to whom love had been revealed with pain and suffering. The powerful creations of Rigoletto and the duke, the sweet figure of Gilda, were more than characters; they were feelings, passions incarnate, and the terrible human grandeur of all that work resonated in every fiber of her being.

The strong excitement strengthened and ennobled the girl's spiritual nature by enabling her to grasp the outlines of a clear ideal. In her mind, she fused her own love with Gilda's. The memories that were already beginning to fade lost the personal imprint, mixing with many other impressions and new aspirations.

From that evening her thoughts no longer dwelled on the young man who had been the first to make her heart throb. Her thoughts were about a vague, mysterious, immense love, and of a whole tumultuous world not yet entirely revealed, but that was being disclosed in stages, with sudden flashes, quick wounds, wonderful intuitions, lying somewhere between the duke's mocking song and Gilda's death rattle . . .

Chapter VIII

Unable to break through the clouds, the heat of the sun bore down suffocatingly on the August midday.

In the kitchen, a yellow water- and dust-stained cane curtain was lowered over the single window. Standing before the long plank table, with her sleeves rolled up and a white apron tied high above her waist, Teresina made a hill of flour and rounded it with her hands, patting it almost like a caress.

When the flour seemed right, she made a hole in the middle into which she poured a teaspoon of water, broke two eggs, tossed a pinch of salt. Then she filled the hole by lifting flour from the base, always caressing the fragile hill that grew thick in her hands.

As the dough acquired consistency, Teresina had to work harder. She had begun slowly, taking it easy, a little distracted, but the resistance stirred her to action. She raised her sleeves further, applied her arms with energy, accompanying every pressure with a movement of her whole body, keeping her mouth pursed and her forehead furrowed.

The young girl's limbs swelled with tension. The veins on her arms and neck appeared brown on the surface of her skin. Her bosom heaved up and down, struggling with her bodice; her hips, with their young curves, pressed against her blue and white striped skirt. A blooming, joyful robustness enveloped her; her blood was pleasantly warmed by the exertion. Her nerves and muscles exalted, and she urged them on by increasing the pressure of her hands, abandoning herself to the physical well-being of the excercise.

She stopped a moment to remove some dough from her arms, holding her hands high, observing her veins disappear in that position, dying into solid white flesh.

From a hole in the curtain a sunbeam fell directly on the girl's hair, forming a luminous frame around her head that highlighted her hair cascading down to her shoulders and the little curls lightly dusted with flour bouncing between her eye and ear.

She kept working, kneading, smoothing the dough, which took on a shiny appearance and became a shade of warm, pale yellow; then with a large piece of cane that Teresina had hammered a nail into, she began the difficult operation of rolling it out, slowly, carefully, in order not to break it, taking care that it was all of equal thickness.

When it was almost as thin and compact as a piece of paper, raising the cane with an expert movement the girl slapped the dough on the table. As she smoothed the dough, she sang from the satisfaction that work well done inspires.

At this point the judge's wife appeared at the door of the kitchen: "Are you alone?"

Teresina loved this loquacious woman who had worldly experience and seemed to understand a young woman's aspirations so well. She went to her with a smile.

"Yes, I'm alone. Mamma is upstairs . . . she has a migraine. Ida has gone out with Papa . . . Goodness knows she'll drive him crazy!"

"Oh, not too much. Your father has a weakness for that child. He puts up with her whims . . . and they're quite a lot, really. But don't stop. You don't have to entertain me."

"No, look, I'm finished; now I'll let it dry before cutting it."

She started to go into the parlor, but the judge's wife sat down quickly on the straw stool, saying: "Let's stay here."

They were silent a moment while Teresina washed her hands and arms in a copper basin. Then she also sat down, next to the judge's wife, slowly tugging down her sleeves, fanning herself with her apron.

"It's hot, isn't it?"

Teresina nodded yes.

Not a leaf trembled; not a ribbon or piece of straw moved. From the opening between the curtains not a breath of air entered. The August sultriness joined to an oppressive heat, like molten lead, that took one's breath away. Some flies in the kitchen buzzed untiringly, almost ferociously, and the two women brushed them away automatically, both in a kind of stupor in that closed atmosphere full of the damp, soft odor of dough.

Abruptly, Teresa asked with a wink: "So it's true, then?"

The other one grasped her meaning immediately. "And how! He came to make the formal request this morning. I heard it from the registrar who is Luzzi's close friend."

A faint shadow crossed Teresina's eyes.

"Just shows money talks, doesn't it? Because no one can make me believe Luzzi is marrying her for her pretty face! You wouldn't have to go far to find a prettier one . . ."

Teresina interrupted her quickly in mid sentence: "They said she was going to marry the prefect."

"Yessss . . . the prefect. He's a sly one. As long as he can use someone else's sheets, he won't wear out his own."

And holding back other brash vulgarities for the girl's sake, the woman returned to her thought: "Tell me the truth just between us . . . have you ever thought Luzzi might come to Via di San Francesco for you?"

Nervously Teresina busied herself with smoothing out some wrinkles on her apron, murmuring: "He's certainly never done anything to make me think so. And I haven't dared imagine it. Why would he think of me?"

"Why wouldn't he think of you? Aren't you a woman like the others? And flattery aside, you're worth more than all three of the Portalupi girls."

"But I'm poor."

"Ah! . . .that . . ."

The judge's wife bit her lip, while tapping her foot nervously on the brick floor, looking as though she were searching her mind for something.

And meanwhile Teresina was thinking that ever since they had sent Carlino to Parma for high school and had to pay for room and board every month, there was a lot of talk about economizing in her house—and they no longer had a maid, and she had been waiting three months for a new pair of boots.

Suddenly the judge's wife asked: "How old are you?"

"Nineteen."

"You're young. But listen, do you know Professor Luminelli, the one who teaches fourth and fifth grades? The one from Ostiano?* who wears glasses? . . . No? . . . who swings his arms like this when he walks?"

"Oh!"

"Now do you remember?"

"The one who has a little girl the same age as Ida?"

"That's the one. He has a little girl but no wife, and he's looking for one."

She stopped, looking at Teresina closely. Drawing out her words, not taking her eyes off her, she added: "He's looking for a good, healthy, unpretentious girl with simple tastes . . ."

She stopped again, waiting for her young friend to say some-

---

* A village to the west of the Oglio River in the province of Cremona.

thing; but seeing she was mute and breathing rather heavily with the hint of tears behind her eyes: "You wouldn't accept him?" To get it over with quicker she cut it short. "Say something."

"I don't even know him . . ."

"That's not an excuse."

"He's so much older than I am."

"That's true, but . . ."

"He's a widower."

"Pshaw! For that matter, all men are more or less widowers, my dear."

Teresina wanted to reply: he has a child. But she was afraid of saying something unpleasant, something that would make her seem heartless.

"Well, then, you don't like him?"

"Not really."

"Do as you please. He's a good catch, though. He's a quiet man, without vices, who has work and a house of his own. I've seen it. Lots of walnut furniture and a canopy over his bed."

"And anyway," Teresina broke in, "this gentleman doesn't want to marry me!"

"It's up to you to make him want to. He spends his evenings with my husband at the café and has been to our house many times . . . it's easy to arrange. Providing your father is willing to settle a little bit of money . . ."

Teresina listened, stupefied, with a desire to cry that formed a knot in her throat and made her feel inexplicably angry with herself.

"I understand," the judge's wife said calmly, with a suggestion of mocking indulgence. "You're waiting for Prince Camaralzaman, the one in *A Thousand and One Nights*. You dream about him and imagine all husbands are made from the same mold."

"That's not . . ."

"Let me talk. You dear girls are all alike, you don't want to take advantage of the experience of those who know more than you. There's something you should know: don't look for a handsome husband, don't look for sentiment, elegance, poetry . . . that's nonsense, firecrackers, will-o'-the-wisp. But no! Just don't get big ideas . . ."

"But Mamma," Teresina interrupted with the passion of one who feels he's found a good argument. "Mamma married Papa because she was in love."

The woman's slightly mischievous mouth arched into a smile of such ironic compassion that no explanation was necessary. Nevertheless, she added: "Ask your mother if she's happy. She's taken more . . . Never mind, you'll make me say something I shouldn't."

"And you?" Teresina shyly took the risk.

"Me? Oh! I've had my disappointments. But when I saw the years were going by, I married the judge, who was then a chancellor, someone who could give me very few illusions . . . but he gave me a child every year in compensation."

The somewhat brutal language of the judge's wife had startled the girl from time to time. Now she was thinking about all those children born without love, although the idea remained fixed in her mind that children are a token of love.

"Well, now, silly girl, what do you think? Do you want a summary of wisdom in a few words? A Luminelli who marries is always better than a Luzzi who doesn't . . . or who marries someone else."

Teresina blushed at that new allusion to the prefect's secretary. She hadn't realized she sometimes thought of the elegant dandy and had followed him with long looks as he passed on the sidewalk, head high, smartly dressed in his light-colored overcoat.

However, it was odd that after the announcement of his wedding with the second Portalupi, this young woman looked twice as unattractive as before.

"All right," the woman continued, seeing that the girl was stubbornly silent, "no Luminelli. Too bad. I would have gladly arranged this business. It goes without saying he's an influential man in the education field, has many contacts, and could be useful to your brother . . ."

Large tears came into Teresina's eyes, which she couldn't hold back. She broke into such a desolate and abandoned fit of weeping that the judge's wife was touched to the quick. Embracing her maternally, she tried to console her: "Come on, we won't talk about it any more. You're so young . . . it'll get better . . . let's hope.

"Oh, for heaven's sake, look at this pretty girl crying, deprived of love, when so many men . . ." She made a fist in the air threatening an invisible legion of men and called them selfish, brutal, greedy, calculating. "Look, if you only knew . . . if only I could tell you how worthless they are . . . Anyway, the day will come when you'll understand everything, and then you'll say Giovannina was right."

She stood up and smoothed her dress a little nervously.

"You're going?"

"Yes. It's time for my little rascals to come home from school. Pandemonium breaks out when I'm not home. You know, I have an outstanding method for making them quiet down in a hurry . . . It might work for Ida, but you have to tell her when Mamma and Papa aren't around. It's a real flesh and blood elf. Yesterday it beat my Estella like she was a drum, but if I find it . . . And so little! But when it gets bigger . . ."

"I don't know what gets into that child," Teresa said. "Believe me, Mother is desperate . . . but poor Mamma isn't well. It's up to me to discipline Ida as well as I can. And I can't do it. Papa always defends her."

"Yes, yes, you have your cross. And the twins, that stuck-up pair. Quick as lightning, two peas in a pod, each one aping the other. They're two bodies with one mind."

They had moved out into the hallway and stopped a moment before opening the door.

"You're a mamma before your time . . . Dear Teresina, true as God, I love you like a sister! I hope my Giulia and Bice, Estella and Norina are like you. I'd be a lucky mother."

They felt a tenderness for each other, holding hands, rocking, unable to separate.

The judge's wife, who had turned toward the garden, exclaimed: "What a beautiful lemon verbena! I've never had one so thick and healthy. Little insects always eat mine, those born right on the plant itself, that are the same color and have bluish stripes on their backs that look like chenille . . . terrible, I tell you!"

"Would you like a little plant?"

"I'd love one."

"Let's get it now."

They walked back to the pots of verbena, stopping to look them over, stroking the long, rough perfumed leaves. The girl went back to get scissors.

"I think insects will keep eating mine!" the woman said languidly.

"Why? I'll come clean them off."

They looked at each other and smiled. A calm understanding drew the two women close to each other. While Teresa bent over the plant to cut some branches, the judge's wife fixed her braids higher on her neck.

"That looks better."

"I never have time to fix my hair fashionably."

"Poor girl!"

To the verbena were added two beautiful pink geraniums and a carnation of the same color.

"Do you know what pink carnations signify in flower language?" the judge's wife asked, gently rearranging the stems, her head inclined to one side, her eyes half-closed. "Pure love. Isn't that lovely? If only it existed."

Teresina didn't grasp the irony immediately, but it came to her gradually as she moved through the vestibule toward the door, and a feeling of sadness came over her.

"See you."

"See you tonight."

The door was closed. Just on the point of leaving, the judge's wife stopped: "Any news about Carlino?"

"Good news. He'll be coming home in a few days."

"Well, good-bye then. I won't come back again. Tell your mamma hello."

"Listen." This time it was Teresina to call her back. She wanted to ask her when the Portalupi wedding would be, but suddenly struck by shame, she babbled something in confusion.

Almost as though she had read her thoughts, the judge's wife said: "Pretty soon the celebration will take place across the street. And who knows, maybe soon on this side, too . . ."

Teresina shook her head, laughing, to put up a brave front. "Oh! If you say men aren't worth anything, that they're selfish, brutal, greedy, calculating . . ."

Already outside, with one foot on the cobblestone street, her friend turned around.

"And I'm ready to say it again. But, after all, it's a little like the common onion that grows soft where you touch it, that makes you cry merely by handling it, that has more layers than you can count, that's found everywhere, so disgusting no animal will eat it. And yet we think it's impossible to make a tasty dish without an onion. Good-bye."

This time she really left.

Chapter IX

In Carlino's room both windows were thrown wide open, letting a bold and cheerful light poke into every corner from floor to ceiling. The practically bare white walls reflected the sunbeams in the brightness of the splendid morning.

The young man had arrived the previous evening. He had grown tall, imperious, with the beginning of a mustache over his lip, wearing a little ragged greenish cap over his left eye, and altogether so different from the usual Carlino that every member of the family had been very impressed.

He had gone away rough and awkward in his badly fitting clothes; he never combed his hair, had dirty hands, and was still the naughty little boy who played in the middle of the street.

Ten months were enough to transform him—too much, perhaps, because when Signor Caccia saw him, he frowned. And a real tempest of harsh words and rebukes followed this infallible storm signal when the student confessed he had failed two exams.

But Carlino forgot the paternal fury in the gaiety of his open room upstairs, in the mess of his opened traveling bag, in the rediscovery of old things and the necessity of finding a place for new things.

He was laughing, leaning against the wall, smoking a cigar, while Teresina took his linens from his bag.

The bright light illuminated both brother and sister, bringing out the slight resemblance in their oval faces, hair color, and stature. Both healthy young people, but already different in the expression of their inner life.

Teresina's sweet, sad eyes searched her brother's lively face, descending with naive curiosity along his cheeks to the little mustache, to the line of his strong and muscular neck. She went up to him, touching his cheek with the back of her hand, near his ear where brown down sprouted, and said with a laugh: "How soft it is!" Then she remained beside him, happily breathing the odor of the cigar coming from his mouth until, overcome by a vertigo of tenderness, she suddenly kissed the corner of his mouth.

He pushed her away gently, more gently than other times, giving her a little slap on her cheek. And then he asked point-blank: "Do you have a boyfriend?"

The girl blushed violently, protesting no, no, two or three times in a row.

"That's obvious."

Carlino said no more. He went to stand in the window, blowing little clouds of smoke and watching them with his eyes, now open, now closed, as though searching for pleasant memories.

Teresina took his shirts from the bag, admiring the bluish whiteness and shining starch.

"I don't know how to iron like that."

"Unfortunately," said Carlino without turning.

"This one's missing a button, though. And the collars are frayed. Who takes care of your clothes?"

"The landlady."

"Hey, the red wool cuffs I made you are still new. You didn't wear them?"

"Certainly not."

Humiliated, Teresina replied: "You wore them last year."

"Oh, last year, last year!"

"You suffered so from cold hands."

"I don't any more."

"And your silk stockings . . . These haven't been worn either . . ."

"You try wearing those silk stockings, all knots as big as string. Try to wear them inside a pair of narrow shoes . . ."

"Ah, if you wear narrow shoes . . ."

"Wait and see if I'd wear house slippers like Caramella."

The girl stopped talking, continuing to remove his clothes from the bag, spreading them on the bed and over chairs to get rid of the worst wrinkles.

"What an elegant handkerchief! And 'Carlo' embroidered by hand . . . I didn't make this for you."

"It's a gift from my landlady. Nice, isn't it?"

"Oh, very nice . . ."

He was about to add something else, but stopped. He took a chair and put it next to his sister, looking into the open bag.

"Go easy, don't ruin my ties."

While she was taking out a doublet, a little portrait fell out of the pocket, a photograph of a woman.

"What is this?"

Carlino snatched it out of his sister's hands. "It's nothing."

Then, realizing that "nothing" was absurd: "It's Orlandi's sweetheart."

"Do you know Orlandi?"

"Of course. A student in Parma can't help but know him."

"But Orlandi goes to the university."

"What does that matter? He's dean of all students, the leader of Parma's young people. Without him there wouldn't be any fun."

After a brief silence: "Let me see that picture," Teresina begged in a low voice.

"Nosey."

"Come on, let me see."

Carlino looked at it, enclosed within his cupped hands as if in a niche.

Kneeling on the floor in front of the bag, the girl leaned over toward her brother, her heart in her throat. She continued to beg: "Let me see."

"You're all alike! Here, look at it."

He thrust it before her with the intention of making it disappear immediately, but Teresina grabbed so quickly she had it in her possession. She looked at it carefully, with concentrated, almost fierce, attention.

She was an immensely provocative beauty. The dramatic, studied pose showed with one blow, like a gunshot, the assassin's eye, the sensual smile, the round, soft arms and shoulders emphasized by a tight-fitting dress.

To Teresina that woman might as well be naked. She felt shame and along with shame a vague feeling of anger that made her toss the photograph almost disrespectfully on her brother's knees. It fell to the floor; he picked it up, wiping it on his sleeve, and turned to look at her.

"Beautiful!"

"She's not nice."

"No, quite the contrary. Could be you're envious."

"Me?"

She couldn't say more. She felt humiliated, unhappy that Carlino would suspect her of envying a woman prettier than she; unhappy with the unhappiness she felt and with the sudden perception of an isolation, like a barrier placed between her and the world; a kind of sanitary quarantine where the echoes of life reached her late, ransacked, stripped, mutilated.

In curiosity mixed with a light dose of pain, she feverishly plunged her hand deep into the bag hoping to encounter other revelations.

She found a ribbon of red silk to which was affixed a little dog made of silvery paper. She didn't dare ask what it was. Carlino was the one to ask: "Do you know what that is?"

"No."

"It's a cotillion card."

"A cotillion card?"

"A cotillion is a ball. There are so many young men and so many women. Pictures like this are handed out. Then every man dances with the woman who has the corresponding card. For example, I had this dog, so I went looking for a woman with a dog. Now do you see?"

Teresina nodded yes, and sitting beside the bag almost at her brother's feet, she stared at the red ribbon.

"Did you go to balls in Parma?"

"During carnival."

"Oh, tell me about it!"

She moved closer, taking his hand, fighting back the urge to kiss it.

"What do you want me to tell you?"

He rocked back and forth in the chair, unaware of the girl's touch, looking at her distractedly. The cigar didn't draw anymore. He threw it down on the marble floor.

Teresina bent over the cigar butt, attracted by the aroma, and teasingly pretended she was going to put it in her mouth.

"Pooh!" Blushing violently, she pushed it away with the tip of her shoe. Then she leaned toward her brother once again, with her face touching his knees, with a ray of humble tenderness shining in her eyes.

"Where did you go dancing?"

"Everywhere. In the theater, at the casino, especially in homes . . ."

"And girls were there?"

"Of course."

"Beautiful?"

"Beautiful and ugly."

Teresina sighed.

"I saw the Portalupis at the last party at the casino."

"Yes? What were they wearing?"

"Do you think I'd remember? I didn't even look at them."

"Why?"

"Because I don't like them. And then, in the middle of so many people, they looked like bagpipers from the hills; clumsy, badly dressed . . . I don't know how to describe what they were wearing, but it certainly wasn't in good taste."

"And yet they are always so elegant!"

"Do me a favor. Tell me how you judge elegance."

Teresina ducked her head. He added, laughing: "It's not your fault, you know, but you need to get out of this town, and especially out of this house, in order to know how elegant women dress. You see Mamma, the judge's wife, the mayor's wife, Doctor Tavecchia's sister, the monsignor's cook on Sundays when she puts on her silk dress. And among all these, the Portalupi women seem splendid to you."

Actually that declaration did not displease Teresina. Little experienced in matters of elegance, she lingered with pleasure over Carlino's observation that the Portalupis were awkward and not at all pretty. Later, when as a religious girl she had to make an examination of her conscience, that happiness would seem a grievous sin. However, right now she didn't think she was doing wrong.

Carlino: "I saw the Marchesina Varisi . . ."

"How could you? Aren't the Varisi in Cremona?"

"Yes, but the marchesina was in Parma at carnival time in a relative's home. Ethereal as a sylph, graceful as a siren, with the distinction of a great lady. She always wore a white veil and flower on her breast; only the flower changed. Sometimes white like the dress, other times pink, then dark vermilion or the palest blue. One time she put on black velvet . . . they said it was a sign of mourning for someone dear to her."

Teresina listened without taking a breath, with her mouth half open and her bosom heaving.

"Would you say she's very beautiful?"

"An angel."

"Blond or black hair?"

"Chestnut color."

"Was she the prettiest of all the women?"

"I wouldn't say the prettiest of all. There was lawyer Neri's wife, who took the prize for wealth and admirers."

Teresina hesitated a moment, unsure; finally she risked blurting out: "But if this woman is married?"

"So?"

"Nothing, nothing."

The girl lowered her head, confused, dazzled by a vortex of new ideas. After a moment of silence, she asked: "And is it true women wear low-necked dresses to the balls?"

"Certainly."

She hesitated again, but was won over by curiosity: "How far?"

"As far as they want."

Teresina bit her lip, with her face hidden on her brother's knees. A red stripe appeared on her neck.

"You've never danced?"

"Never."

Silence again. Carlino continued to rock in the chair, with thoughts far away, absorbed in his happy male egoism.

The girl felt as if a barrier had risen between her and her brother. He was a year younger, but seemed so much older; she felt an uneasiness that drowned her sisterly tenderness. She had been anxiously waiting for his return, out of a vague need for affection, for demonstrativeness, because she had no girlfriends, because her sisters were too little and her mother too sad, because she felt alone in that house, alone in the world, alone with her useless youth.

Except that her brother, the invoked friend, didn't understand her. Their lives went in opposite directions; they had different concepts of existence and different needs and ideas. Teresina was unconsciously yearning for intimacy with a male, and Carlino's coldness was wounding, no less powerful for being inadvertent. She suffered beside that robust and happy youth, that young pagan, for whom the privilege of sex opened all doors. The girl did not reason in this way, but intuitively felt a profound injustice, while her woman's instinct drew her blindly toward her lord and master.

A tiny voice outside the door repeatedly called Teresina.

She jumped to her feet and ran out, and going into her room she took into her arms a little four-year-old love, Ida, who already promised to be the family beauty.

Teresa hugged and kissed her with an ardor that, repressed until then, broke out in little cries of exaltation, a strange contrast to the sadness in her tear-veiled eyes.

The little one had slipped out of bed in her nightgown, with loose ringlets on her bare shoulders, fearlessly ignoring the loud voice of Signor Caccia calling her.

Now she was settled in her sister's arms, hanging on to her neck, looking at the objects scattered around the room.

Whatever Teresina's thoughts were, she didn't have time to listen to them. She had to respond to all the child's questions, enthralled by that infantile grace, touched by the fragility of the beautiful little creature for whom she was a second mother.

And besides, at nineteen sorrow puts down roots, but doesn't yet give shade. She began singing in the sunlight, cradling the light weight in her arms, with an outpouring of sweet words, love names, caresses, and kisses. She sang in the sunlight coming warm and bright through the large windows.

Chapter X

Although Teresina found no real satisfaction in her brother's affection (in fact, many times she was disheartened by his coarse masculine indifference), she did enjoy a kind of bitter pleasure in their encounters, when her curiosity could forage, and when she could even explore her nascent, irresistible need to love.

She often went to his room, touched his books, perused some of them at random, the pages where they spoke of the relationships between men and women. She would open his chest of drawers, stroking and putting his ties in order.

She even looked his suits over, counting the pockets that always seemed too many. Whatever could he put in all those pockets?

Most of all she enjoyed being with her brother when he smoked, observing how he held the cigar in his mouth, how he formed white clouds and little blue rings. They made her cough, but she wanted to stand up to the hot, strong-smelling puffs he blew in her face. Bending over him with a sudden motion, she played with his steel watchchain, making the empty pendant spring open, and she asked:

"Why don't you put something in it?"

Her secret desire was to possess a pendant where she could keep a lock of hair or a portrait.

Sometimes she questioned him about his friends, who they

were, how many, what their names were. She found out he had two intimate friends, both students at the high school: one small, unattractive, scarred by chicken pox, who played the guitar and was named Edmondo; the other tall, strong, with curly hair, a gold-colored mustache, called Franceschino.

It made her mad. She wanted the name Edmondo to belong to the handsome young man with the gold-colored mustache.

Was Orlandi also his friend? Yes, Orlandi also. Though a little less; there was the difference of their ages. Orlandi was twenty-six or -seven, maybe more. He was enrolled in a law course, but he never attended class. You could find him anywhere but at the university.

"Is he bad, then?" Teresina asked.

"A bad student, yes, but a not a bad person. He's very talented and generous, but he likes to have a good time. That's natural."

All this basically uninteresting information was greedily absorbed by Teresina. She populated her virgin fantasy with the images of all these unknown men, and little by little came to feel she knew them and that they were truly her friends.

Sewing beside the window in the semidarkness of the room, she imagined the happy young people meeting, how they would laugh and make noise. And before her, in the totally dark and closed Varisi mansion, she imagined she saw the beautiful marchesina pass with a luminous aureole, dressed in white with a black velvet flower on her breast.

Amid these reveries a shout from Ida, a complaint from her mother, would brutally waken her, and with no transition she would pass directly into long economic jeremiads recited by Signora Soave in her resigned voice. There were no more sheets in the wardrobe, the twins needed dresses, the copper pans could no longer be used without soldering. And Carlino cost so much! . . .

Nevertheless, what could you do? The only male needed a good education, and with an education came all the rest.

Teresina had these discourses in her bone marrow; they made up part of her daily food; she breathed them in the air.

Then, when Signor Caccia thundered against the women's extravagances, lecturing them on modesty, humility, silent activity within the domestic walls, obedience to the stronger sex, the spontaneous acknowledgment of their duties in relation to the rights of men, then the girl felt so small, almost demeaned, that she would remain despondent for the rest of the day. And the deeper the tired voice of her mother penetrated, the better she understood the dull, melancholy look in her eyes.

Teresina felt a tenderness, a veneration for her mother, and her mother returned it with a sad affection, full of implied sorrow. They had never exchanged confidences. They didn't have the temperament for it, perhaps even lacked the opportunity to begin. However, in times of rest during Ida's naps or absences, when the two women sat next to the eternal window, their silence had a voice.

After Carlino's return, a breath of new life flowed through the house, but its flow was circumscribed, not part of their lives. Sometimes it was a song sung at the top of his lungs in his large sunny room; at other times it was the hurried footsteps and subdued laughter of two or three friends who came to find the student, and who passing by the open door to the parlor would greet the women in a tearing hurry and run off, clumsy and shy.

Carlino's bamboo cane, Carlino's cigar, the white spats Carlino wore in imitation of the elegant gentlemen of Parma were everywhere. And Carlino went hunting. His rifle propped in a corner in the kitchen was cause for Signora Soave's continual fright, just as torn jackets, mud-splattered trousers, and handkerchiefs cut in half made work and worry for Teresina.

That young man of eighteen, the only male, the hope of the future, unfeelingly absorbed the entire family.

When he retired to his room to study, there was general silence; even Ida had to be on her best behavior, because the two exams that Carlino would have to retake in October were now the most important issues concerning the tax collector's household.

The father, a presumptuous man of little account who hid his own nothingness in a haughty and gruff mien, observant of old aristocratic customs, common little tyrant, had already established the absolute dominion of the stronger sex.

Carlino found the ground prepared, no resistance, no struggle; he led the comfortable life of a pasha.

However, he was a good son. Many times when he entered the parlor where his mother and sister were sewing, buried under a mountain of material, he would grab them both around the neck, and taking Teresina by the waist, would drag her to the porch, whistling a waltz.

And Teresina, red-faced, hair straggling, eyes shining, and a tingling over her whole body, would shout: "Stop it! Stop it!"

One day he told her, "Sis, today I'm going to eat watermelon."

"Today when?"

"After dinner."

"Where?"

"At Signora Letizia's, Orlandi's aunt who has a nice watermelon patch not far from here, on the road to the fountain. Do you want to come, too?"

"Oh! . . . but I don't know Signora Letizia."

"Certainly you know her. You see her in church on Sundays in the third pew on the right. All through Mass she worries whether her nephew is in church or not. She knows you; she told me you seem like a good girl, and I could bring you to visit her if I wanted to sometime."

"No, no," it was Teresina's turn to speak. "I don't know her."

Toward six in the evening, while Carlino was putting on his hat, someone knocked at the door, and there stood Signora Letizia with a black veil on her head and a mantilla on her arm.

Signora Soave invited her in, but it was the first time they had spoken and a certain shyness restrained her; they stood at the door.

Signora Letizia explained that, passing by, she had decided to stop and ask if Teresina could go with them.

The embarrassed girl was listening, torn between two equally strong desires. Signora Letizia added: "She'll keep me company as we walk."

Teresina's mother wanted her to go upstairs and change her dress.

"Why, no! We're going in the country. No one will see us." She took the girl's hand and tucked it gently under her arm.

The twins looked on with envy. Teresina noticed them and felt very unhappy. She wanted to stay, but how could she?

The twins, growing older (they were now twelve), harbored feelings of jealousy for that sister everyone loved and who enjoyed some small advantages as older sister.

She asked to be forgiven this involuntary diversion, embracing them tenderly, but one of them pushed her away and the other one turned her back.

With a heavy heart, Teresina started out with Signora Letizia. She wasn't yet out the door when Ida came screaming from the garden and clung to her.

Teresina turned back, excusing herself with the woman, resigned to returning to her position of Cinderella, seeing a wicked smile of delight on the twins' faces.

"How capricious!" Carlino said, taking the little girl by her shoulders and making her pirouette backward. Then he closed the door.

Teresina started out utterly unenthusiastic about the walk. She would have preferred to stay home and not see the twins pout or hear Ida screaming.

However, once she was out of the neighborhood, facing the beautiful road spread out as far as one could see, under the reddish sky of the fiery sunset, in the calm of the silent plain, she was taken by the sweet feeling of well-being that flooded over her in those rare moments when she "acted the lady" (her expression). When they reached the last houses of town, Orlandi appeared out of nowhere and, with Carlino, preceded the two women. It was the first time Teresina found herself with Orlandi, the first time she had a good look at him.

Tall and well built, his bearing had the graceful and proud nonchalance of someone perfectly well balanced. His every move-ment responded admirably to his well-proportioned frame. His face of a pale bronze color, with its very even features, stood out clearly from his black, short, curly beard; he had the high forehead of a poet, with a vein that stood out under the slightest pulse of joy or anger. His mouth, often open, cut the black gloom of the beard with a blood-red arc, and his whole face lit up with the gaiety of his laugh, where thoughtlessness, goodness, skepticism alternated with unusual mobility. His large, audacious eyes were very beautiful, and with their mobile, changing look they reflected the same fluc-tuating variations of his smile—variations that gave those features an almost irresistible fascination, the only possible explanation for the ardent sympathy Orlandi aroused in both women and men.

He was a great talker. He didn't say extraordinary things, but he always dressed his thoughts in a lively, spontaneous form more fascinating than persuasive. His friends predicted a brilliant career as a lawyer.

As they walked, Signora Letizia talked about her nephew, her favorite subject, one of the few the good woman had at her disposal.

Further on, they came to a modest little piazza opening to the left, the Madonna della Fontana.

"Shall we go in for a minute?" Signora Letizia asked.

"You'll be late," her nephew shouted without turning.

Signora Letizia and Teresina entered anyway, leaving the two young men outside.

The woman showed the girl the work she had done for the church. A lace altar cloth embroidered to represent the main scenes of the Passion, a veil of iris-colored silk that had been her wedding dress, and plain altar cloths and hangings for the pillars—all placed somewhat high off the floor because of dogs.

"Let's visit the Madonna."

The Madonna, with her miraculous fountain, was in a small choir below the main altar. They went down by a stairway that led directly to the circular chapel, a lovely little chapel painted in bright colors, with a well in the middle and two windows from which came the smell of basil from the curate's garden, mixing with the faded odor of dry flowers yellowing on the altar.

Teresa, who almost never left her house, and as for churches never ventured further than the nearest one, San Francesco, looked around with pleasure, breathing the cool perfumed air, looking at the pictures. She had come only once to the fountain, and now it gave her a new sensation of devotion, of sweet mystery, of contemplative ecstasy.

Rising on tiptoe, she looked out one of the windows at the flourishing tufts of basil. Suddenly Orlandi's head appeared in the middle of them.

"I came to see if my aunt has finished her prayers for me . . . since I'm sure she is praying for me."

Smiling in confusion, Teresina pointed to her kneeling at the edge of the well.

The young man had climbed on the outer grating of the window to look inside, but instead of looking at his aunt, he stared into the girl's eyes. They hadn't looked at each other before, when they had had every opportunity on the road. Their eyes met there, in that strange closeness, separated by an iron grating and practically alone. Teresina, in the pure and calm dim light of the chapel like a saintly virgin statue detached from the wall; he, bold, in an aggressive attitude, with his handsome face suffused by the purple twilight.

The girl looked away reluctantly, struggling against a powerful fascination, feeling a pang rise from her breast to her throat like pain from a wound.

Signora Letizia rose after devoutly kissing the railing that enclosed the blessed well. She hadn't seen her nephew, who had already disappeared. Teresina followed her, lost in thought, and when she met Orlandi as he came out of the curate's garden, she blushed and lowered her eyes.

In half an hour, all four were in the country house.

Orlandi, crazy with youth and happiness, dragged Carlino into boisterous horseplay. They jumped ditches, broke shrubbery, teased, scuffled, with sharp words and biting sarcasm, drunk on their pulsating blood and the strength of their muscles.

The visit to the watermelon patch took up the remainder of the evening with much laughter and noise, until Teresina suggested to her brother it was growing late.

The return trip was pleasant.

Signora Letizia, leaning on Teresina's arm, would say something inconsequential from time to time, admiring the beautiful evening. The girl was silent.

"We can be a little more gallant," Orlandi said suddenly. "Carlino, give my aunt your arm."

Orlandi offered his arm, very nonchalantly, to Teresina. They walked like this down the road awhile, chattering together.

At the end of the road, Orlandi and the girl realized they had lost their companions and stopped to wait for them.

"I never see you in town."

"I don't go out very often."

"Not even at the window . . ."

"Oh, I don't have much time to stand in the window." Teresina spoke the truth plainly, with her usual naive frankness.

Orlandi said no more, but the girl felt him looking at her in the semidarkness of the street, and that look, more felt than seen, moved her deeply.

At the first streetlights, he spoke again: "Are you tired?"

"No, not at all."

Teresina thought she was too foolish to interest Orlandi. Naturally, the young man didn't know what to say to her when she found herself too embarrassed to respond to him.

At the door, Signor Caccia came to meet them, stiff and pretentious. Teresina let go the arm of her cavalier.

"We'll see you again, won't we?" asked Signora Letizia.

Teresina thanked her, shaking her hand.

Orlandi extended his hand also, which the girl barely touched, leaving her own hand inert for half a minute in the young man's.

Chapter XI

The organ had finished playing *Gloria in excelsis,* the final notes still vibrating in the dark nave of the Church of San Francesco.

While the priest recited the Lord's Prayer in a low voice, the faithful began preparing for the sermon. Some coughed, some blew their noses; the women very carefully moved their chairs so they could rest their feet on the chairs in front of them. The women on benches laid books, glasses, handkerchiefs on the windowsill-like frame. Everyone got comfortable, extending elbows for more room, clearing throats, and relaxing with heads back, noses in the air, emitting little sighs of resignation, almost as though to say: We are ready.

The curate of San Francesco preached badly in a monotonous, hoarse voice. His meditations on the Gospel were neither original nor lively. He himself expected little; perhaps he knew he wouldn't be listened to. And seeing those nodding heads gradually falling onto chests, conquered by sleep; seeing the endless row of yawns, those benumbed bodies rigidly immobile, he, the good curate, rushed the words drowning in his throat, breaking off the conclusion until his sermon was reduced to an indistinct murmur, sweet as a lullaby—sweeter and more lulling than ever on that dreary November day propitious for sleep.

Pressed against a pillar almost as in a niche, even Teresina wasn't listening.

At first she had been a little distracted, watching the late arrivals searching for a place, making their way along the rows of dripping umbrellas.

The women sitting with their skirts off the floor, wrapped around their legs, tried not to move, closing their eyes in mystical concentration; but a falling umbrella, a rude elbow striking a hat, obliged them to bestir themselves and move aside.

When everyone was settled and the sleepers' breathing rose, whistling loudly or purring softly, from that multitude, rising to the high naves like a choral accompaniment to the preacher's words, and Teresina felt almost alone, a thought came to keep her company—the familiar thought that for a month had stayed fixed in her mind, that accompanied her in her domestic duties, that followed her down the street, that lay with her all night, and the first one that she found every morning on her pillow.

At her side, her good mother was sleeping like the others. The twins in front looked like statues. Teresina looked at the back of the church, toward the main door, but a group of standing villagers blocked her view. Then she stared distractedly at the ogival windows through which a weak light entered. It was still raining, and drops ran down the dusty glass, making clear little streaks on the dense crystal transparency.

". . . the day of judgment, O sinners."

Because of the preacher's gesture, this broken phrase reached her ear distinctly enough to make her sit up. She tried to be attentive to the divine word, furrowing her brow, clasping her hands over her prayer book. After a few moments her hands relaxed, her eyes returned to their aerial flight in the high cornices, to the leaves of the capitals, to the dome, and again to the pallid, rain-battered ogives.

An imperceptible smile brushed her lips. Through a strange trick of fantasy she had suddenly seen that big window illuminated by an autumn sunset and with a sigh the sharp smell of basil came to her, just as if the luxuriant plants were right before her.

She closed her eyes, her head swimming. She sat so still, absorbed in the vision, that for a time someone might have thought she was sound asleep.

"Thus it will happen when, through God's mercy, we are reunited in paradise."

The sermon had ended. Everyone got up and stretched, blinking away sleep. Teresina opened her prayer book, afraid someone would notice her lack of attention, wanting to rid herself of distractions through intense praying. It wasn't the page for the Mass, but she read it just the same with a restless ardor, enunciating each word fervently.

"I embrace you, O Jesus, my joy and my consolation. O my soul, created in God's image, love your God who so loves you. O Jesus, if I don't love you enough, light in me the fire of your love that it may burn me, consume me, that I may be all yours."

The celebrant was drawn into the final part of the Mass, absorbed in the mystical meditation of communion. Signora Soave, responding to a request made by the twins, said: "Be patient now. Make the act of adoration."

The *Ite missa est* was received with a stir of general satisfaction. Teresina closed her book, apparently composed, but trembling all over. She crossed herself, genuflected, and her heart was beating wildly.

Just outside the church before opening her umbrella, she looked anxiously toward a certain corner of the little piazza. Orlandi was there, sheltered under some wide, ancient eaves, with his back against the wall, an intent look on his face. The two exchanged rapid glances; and then, when they were closer, the young man greeted her.

"Why is Orlandi still here?" said Signora Soave. "He should have been in Parma a month ago."

Teresina didn't reply, but her face turned flaming red.

She didn't dare raise her eyes, but walked on automatically, staring at the twins' four boots stomping the pavement ahead of her.

It was only a few minutes' walk from the Church of San Francesco to their house. At the door they were joined by Orlandi, who apologized for his audacity. He announced he was leaving for Parma the next day and wondered if Signora Caccia had some message for Carlino.

Smiling gratefully, the woman invited him in. He tried to get out of it, but as they were talking in the rain, the twins opened the door, and Orlandi drew back to let the women pass.

First the twins went in, next their mamma, and finally Teresina, who, more dead than alive, felt her hand taken and a letter quickly slipped into it.

She didn't have time to refuse it or to speak or even to look at that bold one in the doorway who protested he didn't want to be a bother by coming in. A word for Carlino was enough.

The tax collector came out of his study when he heard Orlandi's voice. The twins slowly climbed the stairs, scraping their boots to wipe off the water. Teresina followed them.

That letter was burning the palm of her hand. She didn't know where to put it. With a closed fist she undressed in feverish motions, glaring at the twins, who were taking forever to remove their dresses.

Under the portico Orlandi and the Caccias exchanged pleasantries, then Orlandi went away. With her face pressed against the window, Teresina watched him go in the direction of the piazza.

"Aren't you ready yet?"

"Why do you care? We'll do it in our own good time."

The twins were mischievous; they instinctively knew they were annoying Teresina by staying in the room, and so stayed all the longer.

With her forehead against the glass, she watched the rain. The letter was in her pocket, tightly held in one hand.

Finally they went away. The girl leapt to the door, pulled the bolt, and trembling as though she were about to commit a crime, opened the letter.

> I need to talk to you in private; don't deny me this favor. This evening between ten and eleven I'll walk by until you have the goodness to open the ground-floor window.
> I'll wait and hope.
>
> E. Orlandi.

It was more and it was less than what she expected.

For a month the young man had been obviously, though discreetly, courting her. A formal declaration wouldn't have been far from Teresina's expectations. If the girl had had the courage to question herself, she would have found the desire for that declaration in all the sighs tossed to the wind, in the Sunday anxieties when she went to Mass and knew she would see him there in the same place, in her frequent absentmindedness and restless sleep. Yes, a declaration was awaited.

But that letter didn't speak one word of love. Instead, without preamble, it had asked of her something as serious as a meeting.

Teresina didn't know how to resolve it. She felt strangely agitated. Luckily no one came to knock on the door, so she had time to collect herself somewhat, at least in appearance.

She hid the letter in her bosom, but she was too tall and heard it crackle with every movement. She opened her corset and pushed it up near her heart. Then the suspicion arose that it might slide down past her waist and get lost in the house, and the thought terrified her. Then she unlaced everything and pinned the paper to her blouse. Still she didn't feel comfortable and constantly touched the letter to make sure it was in place.

What did Orlandi want of her? Was it possible that he really loved her? He, the handsomest young man in town!

She slapped her forehead: "Oh!" That oh! was an outbreak of rage and pain.

She was remembering the photograph in Carlino's traveling bag, the portrait of the beautiful woman her brother had called Orlandi's sweetheart.

A horrible mania came over her, an instantaneous, lightning-fast jealousy. She had to ask her brother if he knew who the woman was, if Orlandi had loved her very much, if he still loved her, where she was, what she did, everything, everything.

And Carlino was in Parma!

She bit her hand in frustration. If only she had asked him at once. She would know. But what difference had it made then? And now? Did she already love Orlandi so much, did she love him to such a painful degree that she would cry over him? Because she was crying, not desperately, but with those few burning tears that left a trail.

She wouldn't meet him. Oh, no! She would return his letter in scornful silence.

On the other hand, what if the story about the portrait wasn't true? What if Carlino had made up that sweetheart for a joke? In fact, why keep the portrait of someone else's girlfriend in his bag?

She calmed down.

She went over the sweet, brief history of her encounters with the young man: the first time they met on the walk to the fountain,

her surprise at finding him by the church door on Sundays. She recalled his expressive looks, handsome build, intelligent mind, his
smile like a ray of sunshine.

The sweetness of love suffused her. She felt a new jubilation
running through her veins as if great happiness were awaiting her,
as if her life, tightly shut up to now, opened up to limitless horizons. However, now she needed to keep a rein on her emotions.
After all, she didn't know what Orlandi wanted to tell her.

For an instant she thought about asking the judge's wife for
advice. If she had been there, Teresina would have told her everything. However, she hadn't seen her that day.

Before going downstairs, Teresina gave in to an unconquerable
desire to reread the letter. It was the third or forth time she unbut-
toned her dress, feeling the smooth paper on her skin, soft as a caress, stinging as a wound. And at the caress she smiled, at the prickle
she let out a faint squeal of pleasure, trembling all over, it seeming
to her that that paper, coming from a man's hand and which she
held in her bosom, had removed the first veil of her virginal modesty.

When she went to join her mother in the parlor, she was calmly
composed, but so serious, so full of mystery, that Signora Soave
immediately asked her what was the matter.

Teresina lied, as all those in love lie. But in her heart of hearts
she regretted that falsehood; she didn't even know why she was
silent or why she lied.

With her little waxen hands on her knees, her feet on a stool,
Signora Soave began to talk about Carlino, about the shirts she
needed to send him, about the handkerchiefs as yet unhemmed.
Every once in a while she would interrupt the monotonous litany
with: "You'll remember, won't you, Teresina?"

Teresina would say yes.

"Your father is always complaining. He says we aren't being economical enough, that that boy costs him an eye, and that if we don't learn how to reduce expenses he will be forced to make him quit school . . ."

A long sigh filled the delicate breast of Signora Soave, who for a while had no breath to talk. Then she weakly continued, holding a hand over her heart: "I've asked Orlandi to give him some good advice . . . what can I do. My goodness, what can we women do?"

At the mention of Orlandi's name, Teresina imperceptibly started, turning to look at the large mechanical picture containing a clock. It was two o'clock. Eight more hours!

The twins in the meanwhile were mutely scuffling in the window space until they had to be separated. In five minutes they were hugging each other, making faces at their big sister.

Ida was bored with this awful day: because of the rain she couldn't go out in the courtyard and play. Boredom is synonymous with mischief for children; she began to be such a pest that Signora Soave, with her head pounding with the beginning of a migraine, pleaded with Teresina to keep her little sister entertained.

And so Teresina patiently began to cut some paper men, and then some little carts, and after that vases of flowers and houses with roofs, doors, and windows to open and close.

She was calm and smiling, but every quarter hour her eyes went anxiously to the clock, and with every hour that chimed her heart took a dive.

From the effort to contain herself, she had grown pale. She had forgotten to eat lunch. She had an appetite but no desire to eat. It was even an effort to talk. She would have liked to shut herself up in her room and do nothing but think about him intensely, exclusively.

However, that wasn't possible. Toward four o'clock, she had

to go to the kitchen to prepare dinner. Her mamma helped as much as she could, sitting down frequently, holding her aching head in her small yellow hands.

"Go on, Mamma. I'll do it."

"The twins could give you a hand . . ."

"No, Mamma, they have their homework."

The twins were Teresina's nightmare. She had watched them grow up spiteful, distrustful, giving back cold sulkiness in exchange for all her care and attention. They could have been her friends, her confidants, but instead a barrier of ice separated them. This was very distressing to Teresina.

And so all alone in the low kitchen, intent on everyday chores, the girl was deceived by an infinitude of hope, docilely bound to her chains, learning the great female virtue of self-control, the profound female aptitude of hiding anguish behind a smile.

In her rapid moving and bending, she felt the rub of that letter on the delicate flesh of her breast. Then she would press her lips together, shivering slightly, as though to better savor that combined sensation of pain and pleasure.

Chapter XII

The whole family was at the table: Signora Soave, with two slices of lemon at her temples, mildly complaining; the tax collector, red in the face, fuming; the twins silent; Ida stealthily pouring soup into her water glass.

Amid these familiar faces, these people she called her dear ones, who for twenty years had exclusively occupied her heart, Teresina felt almost a stranger. Love had isolated her, absorbed her with that tyrannical egotism that is one of its main characteristics.

She, so good, so diffident that she was always distressed by her mother's sorrow and pain, she who trembled before the terrible arched eyebrows of her father, had only one worry, the fear of being discovered.

The bell tower clock, framed by paper trees, had never attracted her attention as now. The four arms of the windmill seemed to move like the arms of sylphs, gnomes, unknown deities that pointed to distant horizons. Her whole soul was attached to that clock.

"This broth is tasteless," Signor Caccia said.

Signora Soave sighed in consternation.

"I've told you a hundred times to put in some celery. Did you?"

"You'll have to ask Teresina," one of the twins replied promptly.

"Did you put celery in the broth, Teresina? Did you?"

The strident voice of Signor Caccia had to repeat the question. Teresina didn't understand. The second time she was struck by that imperious falsetto and bewildered, like one suddenly awakened by surprise, feeling a sense of aversion for her tormentors.

Celery? She couldn't remember; as hard as she tried she couldn't recall a fact so simple and recent. She felt like an idiot, between the sighs of her mother and the ironic laughter of the twins.

The girl's dejection was suddenly replaced by terror. What if her father knew?

Nothing could frighten Teresina more. She asked herself how she ever dared hide a letter and yearn for an encounter right before the dreadfulness of that person.

She lowered her eyes and began to tremble like a leaf; she felt she might faint.

Another horrible thought. If a fainting fit overcame her? If they unlaced her corset to bring her to, and the letter, the fatal letter . . .

She gave a little jump on her chair.

"What's wrong, Teresa?"

"Nothing."

She had to accustom herself to that answer. Nothing. Nothing that could be said or seen, nothing that others would understand.

Nothing—so often the synonym of everything.

She quickly decided not to appear at the appointment and to destroy the letter immediately. It was a shame to nourish such thoughts in the bosom of her family, alongside her sad, ailing mother, among her innocent sisters . . .

A deep sense of modesty made her blush all over. How guilty she felt! How shameless she was! What had become of her good principles, her vows of purity?

She recalled hearing several discussions about how a minute

was enough for a woman to be lost; that a girl's honor could be clouded, like a crystal glass, with a breath; and she trembled again, frightened. Her face had changed so that her mother encouraged her to move around, take something.

"It's the weather," Signor Caccia said. "No one can feel well with this humidity." Teresina thanked God her father had no suspicions.

The clock said seven. Signor Caccia got up in a dignified manner and went to take his dose of politics in the local café.

The women remained alone, clustered around the lamp.

"Girls, please be good. My head feels as if it's going to explode."

"What will we do all evening?"

"Isn't the judge's wife coming?"

"No, she has company."

"Let's play bingo."

"I really don't want to." This from Teresa.

"Yes, yes, bingo!"

"Bingo!"

The twins were insistent. Ida also wanted bingo in order to play with the beans.

"What else is there to do?"

"You could read," Teresina suggested.

"Reading isn't a game."

"Tell us a story!" shouted Ida.

A story was absolutely impossible. Where would she find the subject? And the patience to tell it?

"No, no, not a story . . ."

She refused in a pleading, sorrowful tone, as if to say: "Take this bitter chalice from me, Lord." She really felt ill; her blood was pounding inordinately, her head was on fire, her hands icy cold.

Signora Soave groaned: "Just as long as you're quiet . . ."

Teresina resigned herself to playing bingo.

The numbers, often incomprehensible, often even wrong, came slowly from her lips. She had fallen into her amorous reveries again. She saw handsome, seductive Orlandi asking her the favor of one word, no more than one. What harm was there in that? Who would know?

A gentle indolence took over her thoughts. After all, it wasn't she who had sought him out.

This last excuse, the most feeble, had the power to calm her. She called out the numbers in a clear, loud voice, reacting with sudden courage, glancing quickly at the clock.

It was eight-thirty.

At nine it began to strike.

Ida was sleepy. It was time to carry her upstairs, to undress and put her to bed. The little one hugged her tightly around her shoulders. She wanted Teresina to sleep next to her. Teresina put her head on the little pillow and pretended to sleep.

What if she really went to sleep there in the cradle, unconscious and serene like Ida?

Footsteps in the street made her jump. My goodness, it was he! No, it wasn't.

The twins were undressing; Signora Soave was waiting for her husband's return. Like a soul in torment she ran from one to the other, hoping to appear casual, but as time went by she was overcome by nervous tremors.

At ten o'clock the door was locked after the master of the house came home, and the couple retired to their room. It was the decisive moment.

Slouching on a chair, with her eyes fixed on the twins' bed, Teresina repeated: "I won't go down, I won't go down." But her sharp ears heard every footstep in the street. She now thought she heard the step that beat a slow cadence like a wordless call.

"I'm not going down. Oh! Certainly, I'm not going down." So she repeated in order to convince herself she had made the right decision.

Suddenly she took the lamp, gave a final glance at the sleeping twins, and slipped down the stairs, weightless as a shadow.

On the last step she stopped, hid the lamp behind a pillar and felt her way through the dark parlor.

She said again: "I won't talk to him, I'll merely look to see if he's there."

Without running into any furniture, she went to the window and opened it.

"Thank you." Orlandi grabbed her hands and squeezed them passionately.

The girl replied neither to the squeeze nor to the thanks, but she was shaking so that Orlandi smiled a little before he went on: "I was too bold, forgive me . . . if I thought I made you unhappy . . ."

Teresa shook her head.

"No? . . . Perhaps not unhappy, but certainly I've given you a worry. Oh! Reassure me. Tell me your kindness to me won't cause you a problem with your family . . ."

Teresina tried to say something, but being unable, she gently squeezed the hands imprisoning hers.

Orlandi was filled with joy. "Are we alone?"

"Yes."

A brief silence followed. The young man also seemed shamed by his frankness. Finally, coming as near as he could, with his face halfway through the grating of the window, he said in a low voice: "Do you know what I want to tell you?"

Teresina began to tremble again.

"You can't guess?"

Instinctively, as though approaching danger, she wanted to pull her hands back.

"You can't guess? . . ." the young man repeated, squeezing them harder. "You haven't noticed anything? . . . You don't know I love you?"

Hearing these words so new to her, the girl stiffened. From the young man's hands rose a feeling of rapture that filled her whole being.

"Is this the first time a man has talked to you like this?"

"Oh, yes!"

So innocent, so wistful, and at the same time so dismayed was that exclamation that Orlandi went on, carried away: "I love you, I love you!"

It was raining. Orlandi was soaked from head to foot. Teresina also felt the rain on her burning face. Under a pale lamp the street glistened, full of puddles. Almost all the nearby houses were immersed in darkness. Only in one of Calliope's windows did a light flicker.

"Tell me something . . . have I offended you?"

"No, Signor . . ."

That "Signor" made Orlandi smile again. He hadn't been able to understand the girl's consternation. He wasn't accustomed to it. However, as he gradually became used to it he found it titillating, while at the same time a wave of unusual tenderness flooded his heart.

"One word more . . . will you allow me to love you?"

"Oh, dear . . ."

"May I?"

He wanted to add it would be a noble, pure love, but he realized it was pointless to say that. Teresa wouldn't be able to imagine any other.

"I'm afraid."

This also made the young man smile, but an indulgent smile like a caress, the sympathy of the strong.

"Dear, don't you trust me?"

He caressed her hands sweetly, first the backs, then the palms, squeezing her fingers one by one. They couldn't see each other well in that darkness where only the outlines of their shapes appeared, but they looked at one other intensely, each drawn to the other.

Orlandi spoke again of his love. Since he was leaving tomorrow, he said, he would be happy if he could carry away one word of hope; he would write from Parma, and asked her to reply.

Stammering in monosyllables, the girl declared she wouldn't be able to receive his letters.

"Why not?"

"If my father knew!"

"He won't know."

"I don't go out alone."

"Just talk to the postman. He's a good man, he'll help us. You just have to be ready when he passes by, that's all . . . here at this window. It's not difficult."

Teresina didn't want to. Orlandi was eloquent and ingratiating. He demonstrated so clearly how inconsolable he would be if she refused that in the end she consented.

Unsteady, limping footsteps echoed in the empty street, going toward the piazza.

"For the love of heaven!" Frightened, Teresina started to close the window.

"No, wait . . . let me see you . . ."

The girl had already begun to close the window, murmuring through the opening, "Get away from the window, for heaven's sake."

"Wait a minute. It's Caramella."

The cripple passed on by, and Orlandi, pretending indifference, began to carefully skirt the path as if to avoid getting his feet wet. When Caramella was far enough away not to arouse suspicion, Orlandi came back to the window and begged her for "a final word . . ."

Teresina reopened the window.

"Tell me you love me, too!"

Teresina didn't say it, but she sighed and trembled and squeezed the young man's hands so sweetly that he asked no more.

"Good night."

"Good night."

"Think of me . . ."

An eloquent, lengthy silence.

"Addio."

"Addio."

However, neither made a move.

"I'll be back soon."

"Yes."

Another footstep in the distance settled it. Throwing his soaked cloak over his shoulders, Orlandi gave the girl's hands another squeeze and went away.

Leaving the window, Teresina had to lean against the wall for support. Her cheeks, neck, arms were wet from rain, and yet she was burning. The lamp behind the pillar was guttering. She went up the stairs slowly, carefully, but no longer fearfully, amazed by her feeling of strength.

The whole house was quiet. The twins slept, snoring lightly, blankets up to their ears.

Teresina fell on her knees beside her bed with her forehead resting on the pillow in an ecstasy of love, with an immense need to raise her heart to God, to make him witness to her feelings, to bless and purify them in ardent prayer. Heaven, for her, was the point of departure for every wonderful thing, and to heaven she sent her new, chaste, trustful prayers.

She thanked God for a grace received, for an unexpected happiness. She felt her life duplicated, another being palpitated within her, giving her the strange sensation of thinking two thoughts at once.

She was loved! She loved!

She undressed quickly, forgetting everything and everyone: her terrifying father, her good mother, Ida who in a few hours would be awake and needing her care. A powerful manifestation of love completely absorbed her. God and Orlandi.

In bed with her eyes wide open, her body stock-still, the letter next to her breast, she went over every word, every caress, everything about the evening.

And she was happy.

Sleep was the furthest thing from her mind. If she could have slept she wouldn't have wanted to, so as not to be separated from her happy thoughts.

She was a little sorry she hadn't known what to say, hadn't asked for a better explanation, hadn't told him she would love him forever. Above all she was sorry she hadn't asked him his Christian name.

What was Orlandi's name? On the signature on the letter, before the family name, was the initial E. Maybe Edmondo, like her brother's friend? Maybe Enrico? Edoardo would be nice, or Edgardo, or even Eugenio.

Kissing the letter tenderly several times, she talked to it as if to a person, improvising songs and poems, finding all the words she had vainly invoked at the window an hour earlier.

She felt good all over, body and soul and heart. A sweet harmony ran between her thoughts and feelings; she was fully aware of her youth and health. She was healthy and happy.

Hugging herself, she felt a new pleasure in her flesh and an exalting lightness in the essence of her being.

Sleep never came, but in a delightful half-awake state she dreamed, murmuring words of love. Opening the letter on her pillow, she lay face down on it, breathing deeply.

Chapter XIII

Teresina thought of nothing but Orlandi day and night, completely sacrificing all other affections, and feeling no remorse about it.

On the contrary, she seemed to have found her true way, the single reason for existence. What were these other divisive, imperfect loves in comparison to the love that wholly captivated her body and soul?

Why had she loved her mother so much but had never spent nights dreaming of her? And loved her little sister very much, but didn't tremble at the memory of her caresses? What was new and different about her love for Orlandi, for this stranger who in a few days had displaced her older affections?

She had never forgotten the deep emotions aroused by *Rigoletto*, but now she understood them better, understood the terrible love that leads to death. Nor did this understanding make her sad. At dawn, happy with love, she could only have sweet thoughts.

Like a woman initiated in the mysteries of passion, she sentimentally sang "Tutte le feste al tempio," but with the happy face of one who feels loved and has no fear of deception.

In truth, her life was enriched by an inexhaustible fountain of joy. When she sat in the window space, busy for hours with mending clothes, who could stop her going over her talk with Orlandi in her imagination a hundred, a thousand times, until she was completely satiated?

And now, yes, Luzzi could pass by the Portalupis' windows with impunity; she would smile.

She also smiled one morning when Professor Luminelli walked by swinging his arms.

How ugly they all were compared to Orlandi! Surely everyone must have noticed her high good fortune. Many times she wanted to shout: Oh, listen, Orlandi loves me!

At the same time, she had the prudence of a serpent not to betray her secret. Once or twice a day she shut herself up in her room to read and kiss his letter, then going out calmly as though defying the universe.

She felt stronger, less humble. If Orlandi loved her and had chosen her from so many other girls, it meant she wasn't exactly the nothing she had always believed. Vanity could not flower in her exquisitely loving heart, but a naive satisfaction made her face shine with a beauty that belonged to happy people.

Her always lovely smile now sparkled. Her eyes were brighter, more secure. In the movement of her bust and the rapid lifting of her chest, the woman appeared through the virgin's stiffness.

Thinking about the judge's wife's pessimism regarding men and love, Teresina concluded the poor woman had never been loved. If only once she had seen Orlandi's eyes as Teresina had seen them, fixed, eloquent, moist with repressed ardor, if she had heard that passionate voice, if her hands had felt the grip that penetrated to her bones and that she would never forget, she might not have spoken so badly about men.

Certainly there were evil men, but no evil could hide behind Orlandi's clear gaze.

After a few days of watching for the postman every morning,

she received a letter. It was a real love letter this time, with ardent words that made her dizzy. A whole new world was opened to her soul and to her senses.

Although her character, education, and lifestyle had made her an utterly prosaic young woman, poetic ideas gushed from her imagination under the blaze of new feelings.

Evenings, between the little girls' monotonous buzz, her mother's complaints, the slowness of the hours on the picture clock, she would feel oppressed by desires and crazy aspirations, and she would go out into the courtyard and stay there for ten or fifteen ecstatic minutes to enjoy the isolation that allowed her to devote herself entirely to him. Neither cold nor wind nor frost bothered her. She would walk along the damp sand in the lanes, hair exposed to the night dew, eyes turned skyward, searching among the myriad stars for a combination that formed the letter E.

And when that burning letter appeared in the blue immensity, a wave of emotion would rush to her heart like a promise, a prophecy, an indelible sign of the greatness of her love.

Now she knew Orlandi's first name—Egidio. Not one of the names she had at first imagined, not even a common name. She knew no one by that name; she couldn't even say it was beautiful. Yet after pronouncing it a dozen times, thinking of Orlandi, it seemed the sweetest name in the world.

Not only did she compose that name with stars. When she had to stay in the kitchen by the fire like a solitary Cinderella, she traced his name in the ashes with a twig.

Behind the shutters, in corners of rooms, on the margin of calendars, everywhere a pencil would reach, E's appeared with caressing flourishes.

On her bedroom door, next to her bed where no one could see it, a capital E was entwined with a T, and every evening before getting into bed she would kiss the monogram as she would have kissed a holy image.

All her actions were involuntary, dictated by her predominant thought. She moved and talked as though Orlandi might be watching. Sometimes she smiled into space, imagining his dear face before her eyes. She began questioning him, asking his opinion. The illusion was so vivid that some evenings while undressing she cried out in fright, imagining Orlandi was there.

The young man could have appeared in any place or at any time without surprising her, because he was always with her. In fact, she was amazed that her powerful invocations didn't actually cause him to materialize.

They often wrote each other. By now these letters formed a little book impossible to hide in her bosom any longer. After a lengthy debate of the pros and cons, Teresina decided to sew the correspondence into her mattress. But then she often had to rip it out in order to reread it, and every night she found just the spot to lie directly over her treasure.

Responding to these letters was no small task.

She knew she was practically illiterate, ignorant of every artifice of style, and was afraid of making a bad impression. So she was largely restricted to conjugating the verb "to love" in all tenses.

Her greatest pleasure was writing "My dearest Egidio" in the beginning, and "Faithfully, Teresina" at the end.

Christmas eve, Carlo came home to spend the holidays with his family.

Carlino had seen Orlandi, had shaken his hand: something of Orlandi must still be with him. Teresina circled around Carlino warily, subtly, envying him the supreme happiness of seeing Orlandi every day.

She used ingenious stratagems to induce him to talk about his friend.

"What a nice tie! Does anyone else have one just like it?"

"Orlandi."

And another time: "Are Franceschino and Edmondo still your friends?"

"Yes."

"Don't you have others? In higher classes? In the university, for instance?"

"Orlandi. He's a better friend than ever."

Teresina was jubilant.

Christmas morning while her mother and sisters finished getting ready for Mass, Teresina was already dressed in her new wool dress with a little gray felt hat, her gloves placed at the bottom of the stairs.

Carlino was whistling on the porch.

"Listen, Carlino."

"Yes?"

"Do you remember a certain photograph you showed me this fall, a woman, like this, with her hands on her hips, dressed in white?"

"Uh-huh."

"You had it in your bag. You thought she was pretty."

"So?"

Teresina, head bowed, clenched her teeth while struggling to button her glove.

"You must show it to me again."

"Now?"

"No, not now. Whenever you want."

"I don't have it anymore. I gave it back to Orlandi."

"To Orlandi?"

"Yes, it was his."

With a sudden motion the button popped off, and the girl could blame her sudden consternation on that mishap.

She had been looking forward to a nice morning in church in her new dress, her nice-looking little hat, but it was all ruined. She felt utterly miserable.

In the nave to the right, the pallid young Luzzi woman, fifteen days married, affected a vaporous air while showing off her beautiful diamonds and old Chantilly lace, which caused a good deal of distraction and sins of envy.

No one even noticed Teresina's dress, but that wasn't what bothered her. She was thinking about the woman's photograph.

The three Masses seemed like six. She was anxious to be alone, to remove all those useless clothes, to throw herself face down on her bed and cry.

The faces surrounding her looked hostile. The organ music brought on the sadness of funeral bells. Why was old Tisbe looking so happy all dressed up, with a new cap? Why was the monsignor's stout maid always so rosy, almost shining like an apple? And the mayor's wife, calm, serene, absorbed in her prayer book? And the two Portalupi sisters, basking in the reflection of their elegant sister, also wearing new dresses, confidently expecting the arrival of their prince? These people didn't love, weren't jealous. Everyone was peacefully enjoying the solemnity of Christmas.

She looked at the Luzzi bride again. What radiance! She was happy.

That torment finally ended and they walked out of the church, the twins in front, Teresina behind with her mother.

Carlino waited for them in the piazza. With him was Orlandi. Teresina couldn't believe her eyes. She blushed, then grew pale, and then blushed again.

The two young men approached them. Orlandi more handsome than ever, radiantly smiling, totally at ease.

"You're spending Christmas here?" Signora Soave asked.

Orlandi replied as he watched Teresina out of the corner of his eye: "I came to see my aunt. I'm leaving in an hour. I didn't want this day to go by without seeing her."

Teresina understood. She grasped the look, words, intentions to her heart. She wanted to thank him right there in the church square under that beautiful winter sun, in the middle of all those people who had seemed so hostile a moment before.

Slowly she looked up, excited, joyful, wanting to show him she understood, while fully aware she mustn't compromise herself.

He walked with them as far as their door, shaking everyone's hand, squeezing Teresina's in a special way, almost to confirm he had come just for her.

The girl was ecstatic. The melancholy vanished. So did her vexation. She laughed, sang, danced in a circle several times in her room. She looked at herself in the mirror with total acceptance, in joyful triumph.

From her drawer, she selected two ribbons the twins had wanted for some time and made a present of them.

She took Ida for a stroll in the garden, playing with her, continually embracing and kissing her warmly.

"Come in, Teresina. You'll get cold."

Was it cold? Teresina obeyed and went into the house. Going up to her room again, she threw open the windows, giving in to a desire for air, light, movement.

At the table Orlandi's name was mentioned. Signor Caccia said he was a scatterbrain who was a bad example for Carlino, who had spent enough money for a degree several times, who would never amount to anything.

Carlino defended his friend. He was absolutely certain Orlandi had settled down and by the end of the year would without a doubt have his degree in hand.

The first part of the discussion had alarmed Teresina, but her brother's explanation reassured her.

Orlandi had also written to her he would get his degree that year and the year after they would be married.

That very evening before going to bed she wrote a letter. She kept a little bottle of ink under her bed in order not to arouse suspicion by bringing the ink pot into her bedroom. The paper was taken from her father's studio: square blue paper in sheets large as handkerchiefs. Whenever some money came her way she would treat herself to small English sheets of stationery like he used.

She wrote that she was happy because of the nice surprise, and because of it had spent the happiest Christmas of her life, and other little things girls in love write. However, because jealousy over the photograph of the beautiful woman never stopped burning in the depths of her heart, she decided after three pages to skirt dangerous territory. She couldn't remain in such distressing suspense. She had to find out the truth from him.

She closed with the usual "Faithfully, Teresina." There was no doubt she would remain faithful to him always, into old age, up to death. If she died at the average age she had another thirty years to love Orlandi, and it cheered her to think how long thirty years would be.

Three days later she received a large letter in reply, with double the usual stamps, containing the photograph of the beauty torn into pieces. With this new victory, Teresina's happiness knew no limit.

A faint touch of pride was mixed with the purity of her love. She felt powerful, she became emboldened.

She wrote again that she wanted to see him, talk with him, ask him a hundred things, convince herself he really loved her, hear it from his own mouth.

Nothing seemed impossible to Teresina by now. With Orlandi's love the future was hers.

Every two weeks the student would surprise her. She would be sewing next to the window and see him suddenly appear, slowing down so they could at least exchange looks. What excitement that exchange caused!

When spring came and Teresina was able to work with the windows open, her heart was always on the street, watching for Orlandi to come by.

Passing close to the wall, he would murmur sweet things, and she would drop her needle overcome by delicious euphoria. Only their looks met in an immaterial embrace, and yet every fiber of the girl's body was as tense as though scorched by fire.

She became careless, not bothering to see if the street was deserted before she leaned out the window to greet her lover. She didn't look to see if there were curious faces behind the shutters. All the faith and daring of love was hers.

One time after dinner in the month of June, the judge's wife induced Teresa to take a walk along the river. They took Ida with them and silently made their way toward a clump of trees where it was almost deserted.

The sunset was magnificent. One of those purple sunsets over the Po that looks like fire burning behind the row of green poplars.

Ida immediately began looking for little rocks and herbs, skipping about freely in the open country. The two friends walked silently behind her.

They were close friends now. After Teresina turned twenty, the judge's wife wanted to use the familiar "tu" form of address. They were quiet, the older woman preoccupied, Teresa in the ecstasy of her dreams, gazing at the opposite riverbank.

Bluntly, as was her custom, the judge's wife said: "Are you looking toward Parma where Orlandi is?"

Caught off guard, the girl turned crimson.

"Don't deny it, you know it won't do any good. It's an open secret."

"What do you mean?"

"Like all such secrets."

Teresina told her everything. Keeping a love secret is a pleasure, but confiding it to a friend is still a greater pleasure. Red-faced, gesturing and speaking dramatically, she tried to make her understand how much Orlandi loved her. But the other woman listened quietly with little reaction.

"Don't you see I've found a true and pure love? It exists!"

The judge's wife remained silent, walking head down like someone deep in thought.

"Well, then, don't you believe it?"

"What?"

"That Egidio loves me."

"Oh, yes. I believe it."

"Then why are you so glum?"

"Because . . . I wouldn't know, but I don't think he can make you happy."

"Isn't he a good person?"

"I think so."

"Did you see him during the flood, how he went to work, risking his life, without expecting anything in return? Everyone spoke of him as a hero then."

"That's true."

"He is clever."

"Without a doubt."

"He's nice, handsome . . ."

"Those are his most obvious characteristics."

"If you only knew him personally, how sweet he is . . ."

"I don't doubt that, either. But he's a hothead, don't you see? Full of wild ideas he doesn't see through, and he has no desire to work."

"You sound just like my father!" Teresina exclaimed spitefully. "As though the whole world should be staid, serious, and boring in order to do anything good."

"It's a fact," the other woman went on, "that for three years he's been regularly wasting the money for his education."

"But not this year. He promised me."

"I'd like to think so. And after that?"

"After that we're getting married."

"Just like that?"

The girl looked puzzled.

"You can't practice law without getting some experience first."

"He'll get it."

"Another two years."

"We have to be patient."

"He doesn't come from a wealthy family, and . . ."

"Stop it! I love him."

After this violent interruption the girl cried a little, clinging to her friend's arm, repeating that she loved Egidio, that she couldn't live without him.

The judge's wife softened; she remembered her first loves, the beautiful illusions of her twenties.

"Anyway," she murmured, "I could be wrong. Orlandi isn't a bad sort. If he truly loves you he'll perform miracles."

"He loves me!"

So shouted Teresina, inflamed by enthusiasm, stretching her arms toward the right bank of the Po, where the setting sun ignited the woods.

»»» «««

Chapter XIV

Orlandi's graduation was the big news among the students that year. A splendid event achieved by audacious frenzy, like a bayonet assault.

What could have induced such an lazy student to abandon a life that appeared to be habitual?

There were whispers around Parma of a secret love. The mystery gradually dispersed beyond the river until it was no longer a mystery. Everyone had seen Orlandi on Via di San Francesco and had guessed why. The other girls wondered why the handsomest man around would fall for that Caccia girl, who wasn't beautiful or striking in any way.

They looked her over with envious curiosity from head to foot when she went out to Mass, making short, sharp, sarcastic comments.

"She's nice, though," Luzzi once replied to his sisters-in-law.

"Nice!" exclaimed the youngest of the Portalupi girls. "That word was invented to please women who have nothing at all attractive about them."

Her family still knew nothing, but the judge's wife continued to be Teresina's confidant.

"When do you expect to get married?"

"As soon as his apprenticeship is finished."

"Where will he get it?"

"With the best lawyer in Parma, Sandri."

"Your mother still doesn't know anything?"

"I don't think so."

"Tell her."

That was a stumbling block. Teresina didn't know how to begin. She preferred to wait in silence for his formal request.

A whole year went by, smoothly from all appearances, but troubled for Teresina, who divided her days into two distinct categories: those in which she had news of Orlandi, and those that went by without news.

Every morning she got up wondering: Will I have a letter today? And what pain, what deceit, what a lengthy exercise in hypocrisy to be always at the window when the postman came. They had become friends. He greeted her with a touch of his cap and the indulgent smile of a practical person, of a good man without malice. She would thank him hastily, toss him a grateful look, and then run to hide with her treasure.

However, many times the postman had nothing for Teresina. He would go down the other side of the street, winking and nodding imperceptibly.

This was always so disturbing, so unsettling, as if the ground were swaying under her feet. She would follow him with her eyes, thinking it wasn't possible that there wasn't one letter for her among those many. Whom were those letters for? Who wrote them? Who received them? Perhaps there had been some mistake. Orlandi's letter lay forgotten at the bottom of his bag. Or even worse, perhaps the postman had mistakenly given it to someone else.

When this doubt took hold of Teresina, it worked like a fever. She could no longer see or understand anything. Breakfast, the time to dress, comb her hair, work, went by. The hours all passed dreadfully slowly. Teresina didn't feel well. Her heart hurt as though breaking or her pulse slowed as though her life might be coming to a sudden end.

She was always dissembling, going impassively around the house like a robot, until toward four in the afternoon when the postman came by with his second delivery. Teresina, who had waited for him all day, called to him anxiously, wanting to reassure herself he hadn't delivered Orlandi's letter elsewhere. No, he swore, there had been no letter. Teresina's heart lifted a little at this. Her fear subsided, but a subtle melancholy replaced it, along with a feeling of isolation and abandonment, as if the world had crumbled around her and everything living had departed. She was left alone in a great cold darkness.

They met two or three times at eleven at night in their usual meeting place. And because their love reached the pinnacle of ideal rapture these encounters were full of sweetness and illusions.

Orlandi had the delicacy of a man sincerely in love, one who hides his claws—not out of hypocrisy but because of the temporary fervor. Teresina had the faithful abandon of a woman who has not yet been deluded.

Together they passed through the most beautiful phase of passion—the radiant, unblemished period. He hadn't said everything, and she was ignorant of much; between these two lacunae the imagination extended indefinitely.

Through the grating separating them they involuntarily sought the greatest points of contact, inspired by irresistible attraction; and it was the girl who, in her ignorance, offered herself. It was she who thrust her face close, offered her lips unblushingly, fearlessly, surprised when the young man would withdraw at certain moments and seem cool just when she felt most ardent.

Nature spoke to Teresina in its violence and purity, and she welcomed the most sacred instincts unsullied by any base thoughts. She was good, she was open, she loved. She loved that young man who would be her husband. And just as she placed her rapture at the feet of God in her fervid prayers, so she did not hide it from Orlandi, unconcerned with the deception of modesty, the reticence of coquetry.

From these meetings, she came away with happy memories that lasted a few days. Her joy had no shadows. No doubts about the faithfulness of Egidio, whom she believed entirely hers, no anxieties about the future. One pain only: separation. But even this was temporary. Eight, ten more months, then Orlandi would ask her to marry him, and all doors would open to their engagement.

This prospect was too dazzling to think about for long. Orlandi's wife, with his name, with the right to love him, with the security of being loved forever!

Her love was like a saint's fatal exaltation for her faith. She felt called, led by an invisible hand. Celestial harmonies resounded around her; she dreamed about her union with Egidio like cloistered virgins dream of union with their Lord, mystically, in the soul's elevation that absorbs matter and carries it away. She burned with the desire to infuse herself. She burned with the female longing that urges them all, religious and lovers alike, to sacrifice themselves on an altar, to make themselves slaves of God or man.

This profound desire for chains that torment the beautiful souls of women has an extraordinary will of its own. From weakness they derive the same joys men get through strength, and in surrender they find a greater rapture than men find in conquest.

Another feeling springing from love was the new respect Teresina felt for herself. She washed with perfumed soap, paid close attention to her hands, realized for the first time how beautiful they were, and wanted to make them even more soft and beautiful for kisses.

"I don't understand," Signora Soave said. "Lemons disappear from the pantry like they were bread rolls."

The twins chimed in together: "Teresina uses them for her fingernails."

In her innocent desire to please, she became refined. She wouldn't touch garlic or onions on the days she knew she would be speaking to Egidio. Even so, fearing she might be carrying some kitchen smell on her, she hid geranium leaves in her bosom. She never felt clean enough; she wanted to smell like a flower for him.

The older Portalupi girl was getting married to a subprefect with a job in Cremona. Orphans were making her trousseau, and Teresina, who knew the administrator of the pious institute, went to see it one day with the judge's wife.

The mere word "marriage" made her heart beat faster. She felt drawn by a burning curiosity to see the trousseau made by orphans from patterns brought from Milan. The poor unattractive girls, not very bright and very unschooled, unfolded the linen to show their impressively patient embroidery work.

The director, an old spinster with hairs on her chin, her face hardened by asceticism, touched the soft batiste with her scrawny hands, holding the hem of her apron under the open work embroidery to make it stand out.

"This is a garland of violets," the judge's wife said.

"And this is Venetian stitch," Teresina added, pointing to a nightgown whose top half was made entirely of transparent lace.

The director unfolded it completely to show her students' hard work. At the bottom of the gown, above the hem, ran a flounce of extremely delicate, curled lace.

Teresina questioned her friend with her eyes.

"It's a bit odd, you know, in certain circumstances."

The stiff director, not understanding anything outside her work, held the gown high, unfurled like a flag. Around her the orphans stood open mouthed, watching in bewildered silence.

"And are all the gowns sleeveless?" asked Teresina.

"Oh," said the director demurely, "not those for nighttime."

"Those are never worn," the judge's wife murmured.

"What do you mean?" Teresina whispered, eyes open wide.

"I mean those horrible gowns that reach up to the ears, with long sleeves, pleats across the front, turned-back sleeves and collar, remain forever as showpieces in trousseaux, thank goodness. The others are much more practical."

The director, hard and correct, bit her lip, taking a package of white handkerchiefs, and then another of assorted colors: cream, pink, blue, pale lilac. All those youthful colors together looked like a bunch of flowers, and they brightened the uniform whiteness of the linen, reappearing in ribbons on caps and on puffed sleeves of morning blouses.

The girl looked at everything carefully, head down, concentrating, trying to memorize the embroidery designs in order to copy them, thinking somewhat regretfully she would never have all these wonderful things.

"We also have baby things ready. Would you like to see them?"

"Whose are they?"

"Signora Luzzi's."

"Oh! The sister."

"Exactly."

"Then it's true? She had to wait for a while, didn't she?"

The director didn't answer. She wasn't obliged to know those things.

The judge's wife gave a superficial glance at the baby things.

So many of them had already passed through her hands! To the girl who was examining them closely, she said, "You have time for things like these."

Teresina blushed.

"We make even simpler things if necessary," said the director, following the thread of her imperturbable thoughts. "And we get everything from our clients, the linen, the lace . . ."

"Fine, fine."

"It's done to help these poor girls who have neither father nor mother."

Teresina looked at the orphans standing in a line, and they all looked so ugly she felt great compassion for them. Certainly not one of them had known love, and without love what would a woman's life be?

"Poor things!"

Thinking that expression of pity was directed at her students' poverty, she hastily added: "But this is a good place for them. The food is wholesome, the work's not too hard. When they leave they have a way to earn a living. It's all to their advantage."

The judge's wife nodded in silent agreement.

Teresina was not convinced of that good fortune. She was thinking about Egidio, his fiery looks, the passionate grip of his hands. Gradually she withdrew mentally from her surroundings. Her friend was still talking to the director, and when questioned, Teresa would utter, "Yes, no, beautiful," shaking her head mechanically without understanding.

A wave of thoughts circled her like an isolating cloud. She spoke in broken sentences, a motion of her lips, a quiver, silence, a sigh . . . The last time they had been together, he had said "my little hands," kissing them. Later, recalling that evening, Teresina would repeat "my little hands," with her eyes half-closed, arms dangling, grasping her own hand.

She was startled when the director said good-bye and the orphans echoed her in chorus.

That gently persistent wave, that absorption in one thought tyrannizing over all others, followed her outside into the wide deserted road, among the green trees, under a sky shading into an opal pallor.

That evening while undressing she again saw the phantasmagoria of lace, embroidered batiste, pink and blue ribbons. She heaved a sad sigh and tried to roll the sleeves of her nightgown up to her shoulders to judge the effect of a sleeveless gown. In the end she realized she could never dare wear one, but she lay down in her bed disturbed, beset by temptations that kept her awake for a long time.

At twenty-two her youth was in full bloom: pure but not insensitive.

The mystery of life had begun to make inroads in her mind; but having never had an unpleasant experience, reality was always subject to the ideal. She felt, she did not know. And she tried to hide these feelings of hers like a sin, just because she didn't know they were common to the whole world.

It never entered her mind that her mother could have loved like this, or her friend, or anyone she knew. Not to anyone she had loved for years, bound by ties of habit and trust, would she have revealed a single part of her passion.

One thought that dogged her every night in the solitude of her little bed, in the infinite sweetness of the darkness, was this: What would Egidio do as soon as they were married? At once, the first moment? She had no doubt he would embrace her. Here and there she had read about lovers' embraces, she recalled certain phrases, certain snatches of conversation, and it seemed to her that an embrace, without window grating between them, must be love's greatest pleasure. She would close her eyes and feel a chill run over her body.

However, when the priest of San Francesco church sometimes thundered against sinful passions, when she read denunciations hurled against the flesh in her prayer book, she was overcome by scruples. She then thought herself a great sinner, and blushed with unaccountable shame curled up in her bed in the dark.

Another strange, inexplicable reserve involved her relationship with her brother.

She would anxiously wait for Carlino's visits in order to have news of Orlandi, to hear him talked about, but she avoided his caresses and didn't go near him as before to smell the odor of his cigar or stroke his growing beard. If he jokingly took her by the waist, she would wriggle away uncomfortably, almost as though physically repelled.

He would then rush to mollify her with an affectionate word, but a kind of acrimony would remain in her blood. On one of these occasions, Carlino said, "How rude you are! If you always behave like that you won't please men very much."

She was left feeling a little ashamed, afraid she wasn't very attractive. Nevertheless, she knew she wouldn't have been so uncouth with Egidio. Quite the opposite: she was continually tormented by the desire to caress him, and after they were married one of her most intense pleasures would be to embrace and kiss him like she did Ida.

She would take Ida on her knees and, beginning with her hair, would laughingly kiss her face down to her chin, her neck, the nape of her neck with wild, rebellious curls. However, she couldn't take Egidio on her knees, and the idea that they might exchange roles kept her awake nights.

Chapter XV

Signor Caccia was in his study, haughty and stiff, even though alone, so deeply embedded was his habitual pose.

Sitting on his chair shaped like a Roman chariot, glasses on his nose and a letter in hand, he grumbled under his breath. An attack of dry coughing, as though something had gone down the wrong way, occasionally interrupted his long and laborious reading.

When finished, he remained motionless with his glasses resting on his forehead, a troubled look on his face.

The dull, foggy day barely lit the room, making the four whitewashed walls and the overburdened bookshelves of an office full of official papers look even drearier. The bookcase, whose last intact glass windows Carlino had managed to break, no longer displayed the eighteen volumes by Botta, the color of chickpeas, nor the sumptuous red leather binding of the classics, because it cost too much to replace the glass, and Teresina, following her mother's suggestion, had covered it with green ticking.

The green color gave the bookcase a mysterious aspect, as if it might conceal poison.

Signor Caccia continued to sit quietly, deep in thought. He didn't even hear the noise Ida made dragging a little cart across the portico, or Signora Soave's broken voice beseeching quiet, nor even the two rather resolute knocks on the door.

When the door opened, he looked up and was surprised to see Orlandi coming in.

With Orlandi came such a burst of youth and gaiety that the tax collector wrinkled his brow and became glummer than ever. The young man paid no attention to this, but cordially extended his hand and greeted the tax collector in a free and easy manner.

"To what do I owe . . . ?" Signor Caccia said immediately, rising halfway from the chair with that modicum of courtesy necessary, but still making it clear the visit was unwelcome.

"First of all, I bring you greetings from your son."

"My son! . . . It would be better for him to have brought them himself than to send them. Nevertheless, sit down. I hope you have no other commissions from my son?"

Instead of sitting, the young man appeared about to leave.

"Excuse me, I see I'm bothering you. If you will receive me another time, just tell me when I can find you free."

Signor Caccia blurted an excuse; he realized he had gone too far, and wanted to justify his bad mood: "No, please, sit down. You must understand why I'm a little annoyed at the mention of my son. When you devote your whole life to an idea, when a father's duty to his family is like a religion, when you face all the expense and sacrifice for the good of your children, it's rather hard to see yourself so badly compensated, as is demonstrated by a young man who has neither determination, nor sensitivity, nor feeling."

Orlandi listened to this tirade in the most respectful silence, and only when the echo of the last syllable of "feeling" died in the room did he feel obliged to respond.

"I doubt that a moment of anger, certainly justified, but perhaps a bit excessive, can make you judge wrongly . . ."

"Judge wrongly?" Signor Caccia broke in. "Look at this letter, and you, who are my son's friend, can tell me, if you know, where, how, and when he could make a debt of one hundred lire. And you know he lacks for nothing! Lodging, food, clothes, everything paid."

That debt of one hundred lire did not make much impression on Orlandi. In fact, if it were the time to express his own opinion precisely and clearly, he wouldn't have hesitated to say it was truly nothing. However, so as not to irritate the tax collector any further, he tried to show his understanding of the man's indignation, adding many excuses for Carlino: his age, opportunities, examples, friends.

"That's just it, his friends!"

To make his meaning clear, Signor Caccia flashed the youth a fierce look.

"I haven't seen Carlino for a long time." Orlandi said this simply, without apology, so Signor Caccia began to feel ashamed of his outburst, and closed himself in a haughty silence more stiff than ever.

"The reason I have come," Orlandi continued in a clear, distinct voice, "is of a nature so different from the worries absorbing your attention that I fear . . ."

He stopped—not because he didn't know what to say, but because he needed encouragement.

"Go on, speak freely. I'm accustomed to keeping my own council. When you have a position of public trust . . . Go on, tell me."

He pronounced these words with much dignity, keeping his tense fist on the desk, his face impassive.

"You know I've finished my lawyer's apprenticeship in Sandri's office."

"In fact I seem to have heard something about it. Congratulations."

"Thank you! But as you can imagine, I didn't come about that.

I started with the fact that my studies are finished to inspire your faith in what I need . . ."

A slight hesitation; perfect stillness on the part of Signor Caccia.

". . . at the moment when I come to request the hand of your daughter Teresa."

Having said these words, Orlandi raised his proud, handsome face, where one could read the conviction of his own merits and the great faith in his requited love.

For a few minutes Signor Caccia made no reply. He appeared to be frozen. Actually he was thinking about Orlandi's frequent walks on Via di San Francesco, of some joking allusions overheard in the café, of Teresina's distraction, and if he hadn't had unlimited respect for himself, he would have been angry for being so unsuspecting. But concerned more than anything about decorum, he stopped and, content with raising his eyebrows in one of his severest looks, said: "I'm very obliged to you for this honor, but . . . your position."

"It's not assured," the young man broke in heatedly. "That's true. Nevertheless, this love that makes me overcome the first obstacles will help me conquer the others. Only if you'll give me your support."

"What kind of support?"

In preparing for this interview, Orlandi hadn't imagined the subject would prove so difficult. It had been easy to imagine. Just on the point of translating his thoughts into words, he babbled: "When you have a small sum to start up . . ."

"Oh! And you are counting on me for this? My daughter has no dowry. I have four daughters, sir, and if I had to give a dowry to all four there would be no resources left for my son, who would then have to work in the fields."

The mention of his son embittered Signor Caccia to the utmost. He rose to his feet, red faced and puffing, having decided to break off the talk abruptly. In regard to Orlandi's proposal, he added, "No, my daughter is not for you."

Pale with anger, Orlandi had listened, unable to believe his own ears. Those final words wounded like an arrow. He took a step forward boldly, sure of himself, his eyes flaming, the veins in his forehead slightly extended: "Signor Caccia, I love your daughter, and I'll show you I don't need a dowry. If you will have a little faith in me, a little affection for Teresina, we'll be happier the sooner. It's just a question of time, and I'll have the pleasure of owing you nothing. Good-bye."

He left abruptly, leaving the tax collector stunned.

Signora Soave was the first one to suffer the consequences of the scene. Her husband found her in their bedroom, kneeling before the little wax baby Jesus.

"I can't depend on anyone in this house! Everything's up to me. Work, the household, our son, our daughters!"

"What's wrong, Prospero?"

She got up trembling slightly, seeing that her husband had locked the door.

"Well?"

Signor Caccia stood quietly for a moment in order to carry on in a severe, firm manner. Then, with what dignity he could muster to overcome his rage, he said: "You have never noticed Teresina was carrying on a flirtation with someone?"

A blush of girlish fright appeared and immediately disappeared from Signora Soave's cheeks. Lowering her eyes, she stammered: "You know girls . . ."

"What?" thundered Signor Caccia. "I have to hear these things about my daughter? Are these the principles I've inculcated? Is this the example I've shown?"

"I meant . . . There's nothing bad in that. Teresina is almost twenty-three years old. It's time her future was settled."

"And to become settled, she flirts with worthless scoundrels!"

At these rough words, Signora Soave became very upset and began to tremble again; she didn't have the courage to stand up to her husband, and yet his accusations of Teresina made her desperate.

"How can you talk like that about such a good girl?"

The sentence was broken two or three times by her sobs, which affected Signor Caccia not in the least, fixed as he was in his inflexible principles.

"She was a good girl—or at least you thought she was, to be more exact. Because a respectful daughter would never dare encourage the love of an idle vagabond without her parents' consent."

Signora Soave's little hands rose to cover her face. A thousand distant memories, memories of vanished illusions, came to make her sadder at this moment. She knew nothing of her daughter's love from her actions or from confidences shared, but she had seen it fluttering in the air, had guessed it from her daughter's distracted ways—perhaps she had deluded herself in a mother's blind affection, in a woman's tender faithfulness to the idea of love despite disappointment. She certainly didn't need to ask the name of Teresina's lover. The handsome, congenial figure of Orlandi flashed immediately in her mind, and it was then she covered her face with her hands, sighing. However, seeing that her husband remained silent, she found the courage to add in a sweet, conciliatory little voice: "After all, what happened?"

"That penniless Orlandi came to ask me for her hand."

"Then he really loves her?" she exclaimed joyfully, as it seemed to justify her daughter's passion.

Signor Caccia gave a disdainful shrug of his shoulders. "What do they know about love, these lawless, faithless young nincompoops, devoted to pleasure, who spend their lives carousing, forgetting their most sacred duties!"

Into Signora Soave's timid head passed, like a flash of lightning, the reflection that neither do serious, dignified, very inflexible men know anything about love, and they also forget some of their duties. But not even the slightest part of this thought was translated into words. She suffocated a deep sigh, just as she had suffocated many another in her modest, resigned woman's existence. Then she said:

"He seems to have settled down. He's finished his studies, has done his apprenticeship . . ."

"And now . . . and now has not one red cent. No position. Waiting for clients to come to him would mean using up his wife's dowry. Some match!"

She was overwhelmed by the logic of his argument. From what Signor Caccia had added, influenced by a natural dislike, Orlandi's position was not the most secure.

On the other hand, accustomed to recognizing her husband's superiority on every occasion, she convinced herself he was absolutely correct. Except for the possibility that with his ingenuity, Orlandi might succeed.

"However," Signora Soave said, feeling in her heart all her daughter's anguish, "if he showed he could really do something, if he got a job, a means to create an honorable position, wouldn't you be inclined to give something to the poor girl?"

"It's obvious you have not the slightest inkling about life. You're just a silly woman good for nothing but idle chatter."

"My dowry . . ."

"Your dowry divided five ways wouldn't be enough to feed anyone. And we have a male heir, the family's mainstay! It's for him we must make sacrifices. When we're old we can't hope for help from the girls. The male carries the Caccia name and honor. We can't neglect his future to give the girls a dowry they would take to someone else's house."

Signora Soave remained silent. She was convinced, resigned. She bowed her head before her husband's eloquence, persuaded by the long custom that women must always yield.

The agony was having to explain it to Teresina. The girl had already read her sentence on the frowning face of her father, who deigned to say nothing; but when her mother tried to erase the thought of that love, pointing out that it could only lead to deep unhappiness, she broke into such desperate sobbing, and remained so firmly resolved to marry Orlandi that for the first time Signora Soave had to recognize in her daughter some similarity to Signor Caccia's energy and determination.

The discovery wasn't a happy one right then, as she immediately foresaw the friction their two characters locked in combat could cause. Truly frightened, she asked Teresina if she had the courage to stand up to her father.

Without hesitation the girl replied, "Yes."

"You would disobey him?"

The yes did not come so quickly this time. "Really disobey him . . . I think not . . . but I won't give up, either."

"My daughter!" the poor woman wailed between sobs. "You wouldn't hurt your father and me by marrying without our blessing!"

Teresina reassured her she would never do anything to bring dishonor or displeasure to her family.

"Well, then, what will you do?"

"I'll wait."

So these words would not be misunderstood, she quickly

added: "Orlandi loves me and I have faith in him. Within a year, he'll have such a wonderful position father won't be able to refuse him for a son-in-law."

Signora Soave thought she must be dreaming. Her daughter was speaking with such confidence, in a tone of such unconquerable will. She looked transfigured: taller, more resolute, as her face had lost its youthful plumpness and exuberance. In her eyes shone the thoughtful sincerity of a woman who loves and is loved. Her beauty and strength were at their peak.

"May God hear you and bless you."

Her mother had nothing more to say. After giving her a long look, she drew her close, embracing her, brushing back the hair from her forehead as she would have done with a child, overcome by the tenderness of that great passion.

That very evening Teresina received a letter from Orlandi in which the young man swore eternal love. Mother and daughter wept as they read it.

Chapter XVI

Although Orlandi had promised Teresina to make her his in spite of every obstacle, he had no fixed plan. He obeyed the natural impulse of carefree youth accustomed to triumphing over everything.

His love for the girl was not a chivalric or heroic passion. Perhaps he would not risk his life, but he sincerely loved her. He would have loved her just the same if she had been a man, or even an old woman, because what he loved in her above all was her affectionate goodness, her smiling sweetness, her simplicity. Since she was a girl, and not ugly, this sympathy could have no other name than love.

However, missing in this love was the great lever, the closeness, the intimacy, the communion of the senses by which a man reaches the highest level of amorous exaltation.

When he wrote her that every evening before going to bed he thought of her, it was true. Orlandi did not lie. After a happy day and a happier evening, after the noisy chatter with his friends, the informal suppers, the heavy drinking, the pleasurable and pleasured women, Orlandi would return to his little bachelor's room with calmed nerves, joyful plans, a pervasive feeling of well-being. He would fling off his cap, overcoat, and all the rest and jump under the covers. In that moment of repose and solitude, on the point of separating himself from the day to enter the great limbo of sleep, he would send a thought to the girl far away. Then he would sleep profoundly.

Almost always in the mornings, too, the image of Teresa came to wish him good day. He received her letters with pleasure, read them over carefully several times, smiling, happy in that intense and naive love that made him feel a special joy. "Poor Teresina!" he would say and put the latest letter on top of the others in an inlaid wooden box from Sorrento and go out.

During the day, he hadn't much time to think about her. In Sandri's office work continued without interruption, enlivened only by the jokes exchanged among the young apprentices. Four were grouped by a window, each with his separate place. A huge distraction was provided by two beautiful girls, egregious flirts, who constantly tempted them from their balcony.

Later, because of his nice appearance and easy manner, the lawyer chose Orlandi to deliver verbal messages. As he left the office on his missions, he could salute one of those well-known little faces from every window.

He would enter a café, order a vermouth, give the newspapers a once-over, hear the latest scandal and news, smell the flowers the owner kept on her counter while he whispered some compliment. After all, he preferred this easy and varied life to the sedentary habits of the office.

At the café, Orlandi often spent time with the editor of *Presente*.* They had lengthy conversations about art and politics; they read galley proofs and improvised articles on the little table. Orlandi himself began to write, out of curiosity, to give himself something to brag about, wanting to show that after all it wasn't hard to do.

* Parma's democratic daily newspaper, published from 1867 to 1890.

He started eating dinner at the Aquila with the other journalists, instead of the inn where he usually went. That society pleased him more every day. He felt he was born for the battle of the pen, for the exciting attention. And more than anything, he loved the free life.

Evenings at the Aquila became famous. Orlandi's presence drew all kinds of Parma's youth—the good and the bad; his persuasive enthusiasms exercised a strong influence over them all. Taller than the others, with strong, virile features, flashing eyes like a natural-born commander, and his happy-go-lucky, careless goodheartedness and lack of calculation won him great admiration.

It was during this time he thought more seriously about marrying Teresina. The future opened up a new possibility; the imperceptible sting of ambition grew stronger in his mind. He wrote to the girl: "I've left Sandri's office and a law career. I have a great plan I'll tell you about in person. Be of good cheer. Everything is going well and I adore you as always."

His plan was to start a political-literary journal, independent of every party, not subject to schools or cliques. It would proclaim the truth at any cost, help the weak and ignorant, face up to the proud and haughty, unmask the villainous.

Orlandi was enthusiastic about his project. He wanted to devote all the goodness of his heart and talent to this work. It would no longer be said he was an idler. He smiled to think how little sacrifice this work would be, and how he would be able to do good without restricting his own freedom or boring himself to death.

With these happy prospects for the future, Orlandi wouldn't miss seeing Signor Caccia's surprise when he requested Teresina's hand for the second time and had flung his title as editor of a newspaper in his face like a challenge.

However, it must be said on Egidio's behalf that his finest, deepest joy was in thinking of Teresina's happiness. Like all strong and good beings, he loved her weakness, and made it his duty to protect her.

The girl's life seemed so miserable that the best thing for her would be to change it. This conviction explains his compassionate words, often repeated: "Poor Teresina!"

An all-absorbing passion was of small interest to the young man's love. He didn't need that girl in order to be happy, but she was a complement to his happiness. He didn't desire her ardently, at once, with the greed of a hungry man. He wasn't hungry. Rather, he held her in reserve.

It was only right. He understood the enormous difference between a man's love and a woman's. For the man everything is a pleasure, a conquest; and for the woman, more often than not, it's a torment. What could he do? He couldn't change the norms of society, and he wasn't born for solitary heroism. The idea of denying himself what she couldn't give never entered his head.

Women, on the other hand, are born with the spirit of sacrifice. All he could do for Teresina was to marry her when circumstances allowed it.

Toward the last days of the year he wrote her: "I must go to Milan. I was hoping to see you first, but I can't. The affair is going by leaps and bounds, at least according to promise. On my return I hope to be able to tell you something positive. I'll be away for eight to ten days, depending on the outcome. Write me. I love you and think of you always."

Teresina went to Calliope's funeral. The half-crazed woman died as suddenly and mysteriously as she had lived.

On Epiphany morning they found her lying dressed on her bed, with her yellow kerchief around her head and a calm expression on her face. She was cold. Doctor Tavecchia said a syncope had caused her death, but for some time the poor woman had suffered from heart trouble.

The whole town came to her funeral, even those who had never seen Calliope and knew her only by name.

As there were no relatives to make the arrangements, the ceremony was in a bit of confusion. Everyone came and went as they pleased.

"You come, too, Mamma," Teresina said.

Signora Soave never left the house. The mere thought of having to take the gray shawl off her shoulders frightened her. And then she suffered a thousand discomforts: the crowd made her head ache, emotional excitement made her despondent, she even feared becoming dizzy.

Teresina crossed the street with her faithful friend Giovanna, the judge's wife.

"Shall we go see the bedroom?"

"Are we allowed to?"

"You can see others are going in."

There was much murmuring in low voices. How old was the dead woman? Fifty, sixty, forty-five. Had she made a will? Yes. No. Was she leaving money to the poor? No. To the orphans? No. To girls of marriageable age? Not even that. All she had would be sent to France to an address only the notary knew.

The old story resurfaced. Doctor Tavecchia again recounted how at twenty Calliope was as beautiful as a goddess. There were whispers about a countess who had raised someone's daughter. Calliope was really her daughter, they said. No one knew the French officer, but they talked about him at length, with the sympathetic curiosity that love stories inspire when time has veiled all jealousy and envy.

The dead woman's empty bed faced the window. The headrest leaned against the wall, a holy picture more ancient than beautiful above it, and below, in a little dark wooden frame, three wildflowers tied together like a relic.

"I thought the house was smaller. What large rooms!"

The judge's wife looked up at the ceiling; Teresina looked at the colorless flowers.

"What's so interesting? What are you looking at?"

"Those flowers. They make me strangely sad. If only they could talk!"

"Oh, certainly, if only they could talk!"

Teresina said nothing more, but she thought: "What memories. Maybe she picked them beautiful and fresh on a spring day to adorn herself; maybe someone gave them to her; maybe they were stolen, or better, gathered with someone else."

A great temptation arose to take them away with her. Who knows whose hands they might fall into!

"Well, it's all over now," the judge's wife said. "Only God knows if the poor woman was wiser or crazier than the rest of us."

Teresina knew she couldn't resist the temptation. It seemed to her that from the depths of her casket covered with fresh flowers, the dead woman moaned for her faded ones.

Teresina detached the little frame and without being seen slipped it under the cover of the coffin.

"You're crying now? Come on!"

She was really weeping, moved to the quick by Calliope's story, wondering if her love would finish the same way.

They moved in the direction of the Church of San Francesco, which immediately filled with people.

Everyone from the neighborhood was there: the children of the judge's wife, together with the Caccia twins; the Portalupi mother with her youngest daughter, still unmarried; old Tisbe, who would never die, as though she had made a pact with the devil. Even Don Giovanni Boccabadati appeared at the church door for a moment, reluctantly carrying around his flabby belly, which was beginning to weigh heavily on him.

"I'm cold," Teresina murmured.

"It's a nasty day," replied the judge's wife, pushing her hands deeper into her muff.

"Do you want to go to the cemetery?"

"Do what you think best."

After the funeral service, a group got in line behind the cart: first the priests, then the women, and some men brought up the rear.

A bracing wind blew from the north.

"It's going to snow."

"I'm afraid so."

They said no more the whole way, both so taken by the cold and sadness, with veils lowered over their faces and eyes half-closed.

Few had come to the cemetery. A little circle was formed around the freshly dug grave where the casket was slowly lowered.

"The dead suffer no more," Teresina said, turning her head away.

"No. It's a consolation."

"They don't suffer anymore, but maybe they still feel . . ."

"That's absurd."

The judge's wife said these words distractedly, her mind on her children, who had turned back.

A long silence followed. The two friends started back on the road. All at once Teresina sighed so sadly beneath her veil that the judge's wife understood immediately what caused it.

"Haven't you heard from him for a while?"

"Ten days!" Teresina exclaimed, listening with dismay to the sound of her own voice, for it seemed to her that "ten days" pronounced so strongly doubled the length of time. "That's a long time, isn't it?"

"A long time? I wouldn't say so. It's all relative."

"He went to Milan."

"Now I understand!"

"No, that's not a good reason. He can write just as well from Milan as from Parma."

"If he went for business . . ."

"Certainly. He has all those projects in mind . . ."

A tall priest passed them, well dressed with purple stockings and shiny shoes decorated with large silver buckles. The judge's wife nudged Teresina, whispering: "He's the monsignor."

The girl gave him an uninterested glance.

A little further on, they met Signora Luzzi wearing a strange hat made of gold fabric.

"Look at that!" the judge's wife exclaimed.

But this time the girl didn't even turn her head. Her friend went back to an earlier discussion.

"Your father doesn't know you're still writing each other?"

"If he knew—poor me."

"Your mother does, though?"

"Oh! Mamma . . . I tell her everything."

"That's good," the judge's wife adjudicated. "Do you know why your mamma sympathizes with you? Because she's a woman. Only women can understand love."

"Men love, too."

"Yesss . . . in their way, but never like women."

It began to snow. From the solid gray sky fell white flakes, small but thick, almost stinging.

"Goodness, what a dreary day!"

"We'll warm up at home."

Teresina shook her head, almost as if convinced she'd never be warm again. Her soul was cold; she felt an invincible, ever growing sadness like poison slowly circulating through her veins.

"What's he doing now? Is he thinking of me? Is he as sad as I am?" so she sighed, with her mouth suffocated under the veil, oppressed by an irresistible need for love.

When they reached Via di San Francesco, they saw the postman. He had a letter for Teresina.

"Oh, wonderful," said the judge's wife. "Now you won't be cold anymore."

The two friends parted almost without a word, one to run to her children, the other to read her letter.

"I didn't write you earlier, but believe me it wasn't my fault. As soon as I got here I was engulfed in a mess of business affairs and entertainment, fun and annoyances that didn't leave me a free moment. You can't imagine the life of a journalist, or life in Milan. I've already made many acquaintances; I've found some colleagues, some friends, some university companions. I go to the theater every evening. There's a wonderful performance at La Scala; Wrozlinger is the most beautiful prima donna I've ever seen. Even the dancing is spectacular. I'm in ecstasy like a real provincial.

"Instead of one week, I'll be here all of January. There have been some changes I can't explain in a letter. I've changed my plans relative to establishing a newspaper. Those in the know have advised me against it, at least for the present. However, I haven't given up the career of freelance journalist. My future lies here. Tomorrow, when you receive this letter, I will be at dinner with Countess Bernini, one of Arese's relatives."

That was all. As often as Teresina turned the sheet of paper looking for a word of love, she did not find it. Egidio was enjoying himself, Egidio was happy . . .

Her sadness redoubled. She felt all the horror of isolation. Those friends, the theater, and dancing were robbing her of her loved one. As much as she believed envy was selfish, she envied all those who saw him, talked with him, knew the joy of his looks and smiles, those who took his time, his thoughts, his life.

What was her ardent love worth? What were four years of uninterrupted worries, restless longing, agonizing waiting, sleeplessness, continuous torment worth? Nothing but weeping and suffering.

She looked at the snow continuing to fall slowly, and it seemed as if everything had encompassed her in a cloak of ice. She shivered. A vague desire for death crossed her mind, along with the thought of the poor woman they had just buried.

Then she grasped the letter passionately, with eyes full of tears, with a heart breaking with love and sorrow, murmuring between her sobs: "Egidio! Egidio! Egidio!"

Chapter XVII

Signor Caccia, having watched the funeral from a distance, was returning home, walking close to the wall to avoid the snow.

At the turn of a corner, he found himself face to face with the monsignor, whose illustrious personage he hurried to greet with a flourish of his hat. But imagine his surprise when the mitered prelate stopped.

"My dear Signor Caccia, how fortunate to have run into you."

"Monsignor, you embarrass me. It is I who . . ."

"Your family is well?"

"Very well, thank God."

"And the young man?"

"He's at Parma finishing his last year of law."

As they talked, the monsignor headed for his street and the tax collector followed humbly, keeping to the left, proud of the public honor he was receiving.

"Your wife?"

"So so. Always delicate . . ."

"A fine woman! And the girls?"

"Growing, Monsignor."

They reached the prelate's house. With a graceful and authoritative gesture, the monsignor invited Signor Caccia to enter.

The servant wearing a leather skullcap led them into a spacious but nearly bare sitting room. The furniture was lost between one large window and another, under portraits that presided majestically in their smoke-darkened frames: portraits of ascetic priests with sunken cheeks and pointed chins; portraits of flourishing, plump, shining priests with double chins flowing over their collars; sly little insincere eyes showing the docility of servants in good faith; the entire collection of mitered habits preceding the monsignor.

"This room is a little cold . . ."

The tax collector racked his brain to think what the monsignor was up to. However, the latter didn't leave him in suspense for long. Modulating his voice to an allegretto full of ease, he asked him straight out:

"And your oldest daughter, when do we marry her?"

Signor Caccia, confused, didn't know how to answer on the spot. This had been totally unexpected. Then the monsignor continued:

"It seems indiscreet, but it isn't. Believe me, dear sir, this is our sphere, fathers both, and the honor and happiness of our daughters in Christ is more important to us than life."

"Thank you," said the tax collector, all red and panting, with raised eyebrows, but making a great display of dignity. "Between her mother and me, my daughter's happiness is well taken care of. As for our family's honor . . ." He couldn't continue; he was choking.

The monsignor smiled unctuously and with the most perfect control went on: "God forbid! Signor Caccia, I have unlimited respect for your family. I beg you not to misunderstand me. It often happens that people directly involved in an affair are unable to size up its significance and consequences. Allow me to explain myself better."

"Please do."

"The whole town is talking about the relationship of your daughter and the lawyer, Orlandi. They know Orlandi requested her for his wife at the end of last year, and you refused. But why does this affair continue? Why do you allow your good, honest daughter to waste her best years, her heart, her reputation, every gentle affection of her soul on an empty affair without foundation for the future?

"What is that to me, you wonder. You are ready to ask me what right I have to judge the business of others. But the religion we profess gives us thorny missions. Can I see a brother on the edge of an abyss and not warn him, not try to pull him back for the simple reason that he doesn't know me?"

Signor Caccia mopped his perspiring forehead with his handkerchief. All this man's defects, his arrogance, ineptitude, imperious pigheadedness united with his single virtue—honor—to make it one of the most miserable moments of his life.

Finally getting hold of himself, with a calm and noble countenance, he said: "My daughter . . ."

The monsignor broke in immediately, stopping the hand that was extended as though to swear a solemn oath.

"Not a word in the girl's defense. Who doesn't know her? Who would dare cast the first stone? The question is reduced to a simple dilemma. Either you consent to the wedding (and let's do it as quickly as possible) or you don't consent, and then in neighborly charity, in my duty as rector of souls, I beg you to put an end to this scandalous situation."

"As far as I'm concerned . . ."

"If you're agreeable, I'll speak to the young man, unless you think it better to give your consent . . ."

"Never!"

With this negative adverb allowing him to vent his anger a bit, the tax collector regained some courage. By declaring "never" with such resolve, he felt rehabilitated in his own eyes. It was a public act affirming his authority as head of his family, a guarantee for his daughter's happiness, a satisfaction for the monsignor, and above all a just revenge against Orlandi, whom he now hated more than ever. With great conviction he repeated: "Never!"

"My concern is to avoid scandal. It's not my place to judge if you are right or wrong to oppose this marriage. However, *inter nos*, as a friend, I congratulate you. That Orlandi is a wild one. Now he's got himself mixed up with politics and journalism . . . things you never know where they'll end."

Signor Caccia was very flattered the monsignor agreed with him about Orlandi. After this humiliating exposure, he choked back the residue of anger while he bowed deeply and took his leave, followed to the door by the prelate mouthing compliments in a soft and insinuating voice.

But once outside, away from the charm and fascination of this august personage, the tax collector felt his blood boil again. His family had never been the center of gossip; never in his high regard for decorum had he permitted a gesture, a word, to pass that could offer a weak side to slander. In his limited imagination a spotlight shone on one single ideal: the honor of his name. And to this he had sacrificed every other consideration.

And now? Here he was caught in a mess of disgusting, humiliating rumor because of Teresina. What would the town say? At the thought of what the town might be saying, Signor Caccia could no longer contain himself.

It was true that twenty years ago he would not have held in very high regard the town's opinion about his own particular affairs, in which a *man never loses*. But a woman? Oh! It's a different matter for women. Signor Caccia held this difference as an article of faith. When a man doesn't steal, doesn't lie, doesn't betray, it's enough—everything else is allowed him. Demands on a woman were different.

"By God," he stammered, hugging himself in his overcoat, "we'll see who is master in my house! Can I let our name be the laughingstock of a bunch of do-nothings because a foolish girl disobeys me?"

A little urchin crossed the street singing: "Look what love makes me do."

Signor Caccia turned angrily, as if bitten by a viper. "It's dirty songs like those that make girls lose their heads," he thought.

When he reached home, it was impossible for him to plan a deliberate speech; he had to immediately discharge his bile and his excessive behavior was so violent that Signora Caccia fainted. When they had settled the poor woman in her bed, with a sip of chamomile tea burning in her stomach, the tax collector ripped into Teresina, heaping on her the most terrible threats.

He told her she was a family disgrace, the dishonor of his white hair; by persisting in that love affair she had shortened his life; because of her, her innocent sisters had lost their reputations, and many, many other things enough to make the flesh creep. All said in a sincere tone and with such deeply felt indignation that the girl, head bowed like the greatest sinner, didn't even dare cry.

Also, she had been raised with the preoccupation about modesty that surrounds women, making them all ashamed of love, accepting it as an abstraction, but never as a reality.

A girl becomes tender at the kiss of Juliet and Romeo because it is far removed, because it is written or painted. But she would never dare confess her lover kissed her, and she is prompt to be scandalized if a talkative friend admits of being kissed. All this without hypocrisy, only because of the continual struggle in which she finds herself between nature and society—society telling her to refuse, nature crying out for her to accept.

Teresina would have died of shame if someone could have read in her soul the degree to which she loved. She was convinced she loved too much, much more than allowed by religion and female modesty; this was a great sin she confessed to God. Listening to her father's grave words, she felt lost, without remission.

It was as though those words had caught her naked. A disgrace, an irremovable stain.

She spoke not a word, neither to defend herself nor to plead her case. When her father wanted her to swear never to think of Orlandi again, she bent like a broken reed to the ground, completely annihilated. Her reply was lost in sobs.

But then, the hours, days, weeks following that terrible moment!

She didn't dare look her father in the face, or even her sisters, who had assumed an irreproachable haughtiness.

Only to her mother could Teresina turn tearful eyes without finding reproof.

What long sorrowful silences in the parlor! What torment, renewed each day when the family gathered at the table and the head of the house, whose scowl was heavier than ever, presided like a judge.

Nothing in that dark parlor was friendly to Teresina: not the window she was forbidden to face, from which she could no longer hear Egidio's footsteps; not the clock that had anxiously counted her happy hours. She fell into a deep sadness. Every object surrounding her, every piece of furniture, carried the imprint of the past. Here she had secretly read a letter. Over there she had thought about, wept, sighed over love. Her memories were recent, still warm.

Her father's condemnations, her mothers pleas, the dread of being singled out as shameful, of being unable to raise her head without blushing, had made a deep impression on her. She knew she couldn't bear such a life, and Orlandi's last letter had helped her intentions to forget.

But forgetting was so difficult, sorrowful, spiked with thorns!

What was there to forget? The rapture? So vivid. The anxieties? So compensated. The doubts, expectations, sorrows? They all riveted the chain. Forget five years of one's own existence?

Exhorted by her mother, advised by her friend, she had written him not to think of her anymore, it wasn't destined, her family was against it; he should never write again or try to see her.

After sending the letter she lived as in a dream.

From one moment to the next, she expected to see him appear. At night she dreamed her father gave his consent to the wedding and Orlandi, a millionaire, came to get her, to everyone's amazement and surprise.

Sometimes after a day of torment and indescribable boredom, after having silently wept on the shirts as she sewed, Teresina would go to bed tired, nauseated with life. She would evoke sleep, the only good thing left to her. In sleep she hoped to find oblivion. But upon waking in the morning her first thought was of her lost love, and she was beset by such desperation it seemed impossible to begin that day like the day before.

Yet she resumed it through monotonous habit, the unspeakable monotony of female life, dragging her sadness from room to room, amazed at her own passivity in such pain.

What could she do? Rebel against her father, make that angel of a mother die of worry, break with all family traditions, neglect the duties of an obedient and submissive daughter?

Her enslavement surrounded her on all sides. Affection, habit, religion, society, examples, each had its own snare. She had glimpsed happiness and couldn't reach it. Was she now free? A young woman is never free, not even free to show her own suffering. She must pretend with her mother out of love, with her father out of fear, with her sisters out of shame.

It was worse when she went out. They looked at her as if she were a rare animal walking on two legs. Every woman who had envied her conquest of Orlandi got revenge by laughing in her face, mocking her. The most prudent whispered quietly. Men looked her boldly in the eye.

None of these curious folks took love seriously. They were inclined to find the happy, inconsequential side, something to laugh at, an obscene joke. Love was really just a drama for the actors, a farce for the audience.

Between two young men Teresina overheard this fragment of conversation, which seemed to be about her:

". . . and as for that one . . ."

"She's a ninny."

"I'm talking about him."

"Oh, he'll get over her." Laughter.

In the midst of all her pain, Teresina was aware of its absurdity, but an absurdity whose meaning she couldn't pin down. Just as in earlier times, she felt isolated, connected to the world only through her family, with a great fog surrounding everything.

She felt like someone who never attends school regularly as a child and later feels suddenly on slippery ground because of gaps in his knowlege.

This deficiency humiliated her more than ever now, at the peak of her development as a woman, and the derisive compassion that anyone showed her made her face burn as though lashed.

The twins, who had grown into two pretty young women, flaunted their seventeen years with a certain insolence, considering their older sister already destined to become an old maid. And in fact, Teresina's small stature, her pale, calm face, were enough to make her disappear in between those two giants, who had inherited their father's strong coloring and wide shoulders.

A new series of little mortifications began for Teresina. Torments like slow, almost invisible pinpricks touched her female vanity and entered her heart, infecting it with the poison of ingratitude, leaving behind discouragement and discomfort with everything.

The great coil of her female constitution, the need for pleasure, had lost its spring. Pleasure to whom? The whole world was indifferent. She couldn't admit, even as a remote hypothesis, that she could love another.

There are women who make a mistake the first time and recover afterward, but she felt Egidio was the other half of her soul. Someone could have interested her before; now it was impossible.

She saw death approaching, a death preceded by the annihilation of all her faculties, a liberating death. She often thought about Calliope, and it seemed to her that peace must be found underground.

»»» «««

Chapter XVIII

Thus Teresina's sadness continued, mute but profound, so that during the last days of carnival Signor Caccia broke his austere regimen and promised to take his daughters to the masked ball to be held in the theater.

In his harmless ineptitude, he meant this festive occasion to benefit the poor suffering member of his family, but in order to hide his intentions he had to ask the twins to get ready for the evening also, since their age made it unavoidable. And they did so with an enthusiasm Teresina was unable to share.

With an indifferent eye, she looked at the pink summer dresses the twins were sprucing up with new frills. She, too, had a pink dress, but the idea of putting it on was repulsive. She felt too old, too ugly, and too emotionally upset.

Just a few hours earlier, she had been so overcome by the desire to cry she had asked to be allowed to stay home. Signor Caccia told her that if she stayed home she would deprive her sisters of the enjoyment. At that Teresina complied, stifling a sigh.

She hadn't gone to the theater since *Rigoletto*, and to reflect on her impressions of that opera now wrung her heart. To herself she sang, "Tutte le feste al tempio," thinking of Orlandi.

She entered the theater with tears in her eyes.

Sitting in the box behind the twins—she hadn't wanted to sit near the rail—she continued thinking about Orlandi. What was he doing now? Perhaps enjoying himself in Parma; perhaps he was in Milan, at La Scala, applauding that beautiful prima donna. Did he think of her? Was he already over her? In two months, he'd given no sign of life.

"Look at those girls with bare arms. They're the Ridolfis. Their father bought Calliope's house. We'll be neighbors."

"Don Giovanni's looking at them through his binoculars."

"He can look at them as long as he likes. He doesn't put anyone in the shade. I can't believe he was ever handsome; he looks old and dried up."

"Who's that one with the short mustache—shorter than his nose?"

"Near Luminelli?"

"Yes."

"Must be his brother."

"How do you know?"

"I heard someone say; besides, he looks like him."

Teresina heard the twin's chatter, but she didn't take part in it, didn't listen, didn't look at anyone. She gave herself up to melancholy, finding it all she could do.

Looking down on the audience absentmindedly she saw Luminelli, whose wife she was supposed to be, and who had never married. If she had taken him when the judge's wife had proposed it, she would now be on his arm, they would eat together, sleep together. She would give him kisses and embrace him fondly. The idea of embracing Luminelli brought a lump to her throat. She turned away and rested her head on the upholstered back of her chair. Orlandi's kisses were burning her lips . . .

The masqueraders began to group: serious, cool, and collected, showing off their fancy clothes. The twins entertained themselves by trying to guess who they were.

"That one is the pharmacist."

"Think so?"

"Without a doubt. Don't you see how he moves and holds his elbows out?"

"Then the blue domino looking like his shadow is Gigia?"

"Naturally."

"When they masquerade, they should disguise themselves better."

"That's difficult when we know everyone."

No one recognized four young men disguised in the elegant costumes of Venetian gentlemen who had invaded the stage with devilish gaiety. Outsiders, certainly. But who were they?

The twins went down to dance. The younger Luminelli was very attentive to one of them.

"What is that young man doing?" asked Signor Caccia suspiciously, because after the business with Teresina he was always suspicious of his daughters' love interests.

The carabinieri lieutenant filled him in completely, telling him he was a teacher like his brother and a very respectable man.

After taking several turns with the twins, the young teacher insisted on dancing with Teresina.

"It's a delicate situation," thought Signor Caccia, and as much as Teresina wanted to refuse, he urged her to accept at least one turn to keep people from talking.

They went down arm in arm, in total and reciprocal indifference. He was concerned only with making their way through the masqueraders. Bored and put out, not looking forward to any pleasure in the dance, Teresa was thinking she would rather be alone in her little bed, where at least she could be resting.

"Do you like to dance fast or slow?"

"As you wish."

They made half a turn, bumping into each other and stepping on each other's toes, never getting together.

"Shall we try a fast one?"

"I told you, whatever you want!"

A group of Pierrots swept them away, pinning them against a wall. It was all they could do to stay on their feet. Teresina, losing her patience, feeling her nausea and irritation with the crowd grow, took her hand from her partner's shoulder, about to tell him she was tired.

Precisely at that moment, one of the four Venetians in short cloaks took her by the waist. Luminelli, inexperienced, bewildered, thought she had left him to dance with the masquerader, and having no reason to regret it, stood by to watch. Anyway, he was thinking, they would never do very well together.

Before Teresina could say a single word, the passionate embrace of her kidnapper told her who he was.

In the confusion, turning ably, he could keep her tight against his chest in a dizzy sweep. Through the mask his mouth touched the girl's hair.

"I have to talk to you. Don't say no. Be at the end of your garden at dawn."

A few minutes later, leading his dancer back to Luminelli, the Venetian gentleman bowed deeply, thanked him, and disappeared into the crowd.

Teresina hadn't opened her mouth. She attached herself to Luminelli's arm like someone seeing double, and when he asked her if she wanted to continue dancing, she shook her head no. With a sigh of relief, Luminelli took her back to her box.

The twins looked at her in surprise. Her father asked her if she was not well. As for her, she couldn't speak. She shook her head, staring into space.

"I can see you don't like to dance," Signor Caccia said.

The incident with the masquerader had been so brief, so rapid, no one had noticed. Luminelli took his flame by the hand and returned to the stage to better prove his ability.

"It's almost time to go. It's one," announced Signor Caccia, looking at his antique gold pocketwatch.

"Oh! Let's go home."

Those were Teresina's first words of the evening as she came out of her stupor. She couldn't believe she was really getting away from that mob. The first mouthful of pure air revived her, making her feel the need to move. She ran alongside the wall with her head held high to feel the cool night air on her face.

"What a frenzy!" said one of the twins, cross about having to leave the ball so soon.

Teresina slowed down, but didn't reply. It was the first time she had been on the street at that hour. And in that state of exaltation caused by suddenly meeting Orlandi, she would have liked to walk alone in the dark, in the cool air, in silence.

Her placid imagination marveled at the shapes of a fantastic world she saw.

The well-known houses, the streets so often traversed appeared entirely new. But what impressed her even more than the material objects was night's mystery. That great cold silence, that purity of air and land that became stronger with the absence of people, almost as if nature wanted to take back its rights violated every day in the sunlight.

But she felt the instinct for freedom so strongly. Without realizing it, she began to run again, deluding herself that she was in control, feeling one of the most inebriating joys of her life in this deception.

But the tax collector's voice called in falsetto: "Teresina!" and the enchantment vanished. Father, mother, family, decorum, habit, all the chains of her existence took their place again. She jumped as if an iron band had been clapped on her wrists.

Only when she was in her bedroom did she begin to consider Orlandi's proposal with relative coolness. He had said at the bottom of the garden, realizing that after the scandal she wouldn't dare stand at the window facing the street.

The garden was bordered by an unused lane, but the wall was high. How would they be able to talk? And above all, what did he have to say to her?

For a year Teresina had slept alone in her room. The twins and Ida had been moved into Carlino's large room. Therefore, sitting on the side of her bed, she had every opportunity to reflect and think about the most extravagant or the most ordinary matters.

When she saw the candle was almost entirely consumed and was about to burn the paper, she quickly took off her party dress, put on her house dress and, blowing out the flame, threw herself half-dressed on her bed to wait for dawn.

Toward five the window grew white, giving her notice of the beginning day. She was amazed how difficult it was to get up, surprised to feel as she did. Every bone ached.

Over her shoulders she put a black shawl and went down the stairs shivering, yawning convulsively, with a great empty space in place of her stomach.

She crossed the garden through the dry plants, on the path white with frost, glancing to the right at the judge's house, and to the left at Don Giovanni's house sunk behind a cluster of green magnolia trees.

At the back, on the wall where the fig tree extended its knotty branches, Orlandi was in sight, ready. As soon as the girl appeared he came down.

Teresina was surprised, not at his appearance, but for not having thought before that this was a very accessible place for a daring lover.

They embraced at once without speaking, almost afraid of losing time. The girl, who had prepared a dignified speech, found herself clinging to Egidio's neck, kissing his cheeks, his ears, his hair, holding him in the warmth of her arms with a wonderful sensation that drowned reason.

She was no longer cold, no longer tired. Her entire body leaned against his, was abandoned to that young man's, completely oblivious to everything else. Her embrace gradually tightened instinctively, unconsciously, with only one clear and precise idea: Egidio in her arms.

He took her head, and pushing it back with a brusque movement, kissed her on the lips.

"Come with me. Let's run away."

The sound of his voice shook Teresina. She stepped back, keeping her hands on his shoulders, looking at him, inebriated.

"Come with me. Your father will never agree to us getting married unless he's forced to. I'll take you to Parma to stay with my two sisters. Do you want to?"

Teresina didn't know if he had come with that plan, or if it had suddenly come up in the delirium of their first embrace. However, she felt Egidio was sincere, and she had never felt as loved as right at that moment.

But while this ambiguity flooded her heart with immense joy, balancing the scales on one side, there came up, on the other side, the fear of doing anything an honest girl shouldn't do.

"No, no, no. I can't. I promised my mother."

"What did you promise her?"

"Not to make her unhappy . . ."

"And to give me up?"

"Oh, no, not that!"

A slight embarrassment colored Orlandi's forehead. Encircling her waist with his arm he pulled her to him. "Let's think about it. May I talk to your father?"

"Yes . . . when you have a secure job."

"Just what I don't have."

"But you wrote me . . ."

"Those plans didn't work out. I do what I can, writing for one newspaper or another."

"Why did you ever go into journalism?"

"Who knows! An interest like any other, and one that includes all interests."

He held her gently, searching for her mouth once more, smiling like a happy man.

For five minutes they didn't speak.

"You must be cold . . ."

Orlandi took off his cloak and wrapped it around Teresina with almost maternal care, observing her pale cheeks that bore traces of a sleepless night.

"Now you'll be cold."

"Me?"

He was about to say: I can't be cold because I had a lavish supper. But facing that dejected little face marked by all her sacrifices, he felt a sense of pity. He lifted the edge of the cloak to cover his shoulders, and changed the direction of his discourse: ". . . if you'll let me stay here I won't be cold anymore."

She held him close, happy, discovering new joy in that protection, almost anticipating the serious and solemn intimacy of marriage. It was true she felt the cold. She hadn't slept, hadn't eaten since the previous day. But even the bone-chilling cold of dawn had its voluptuousness: it made the warmth of those embraces sweeter.

What Egidio was saying disturbed her. "Then you'll come with me?"

"You know I can't!" she replied with tears in her eyes, holding his hand tightly.

"Well, what can we do?"

"Wait."

Faith was her strength. Unsure, ignorant, she didn't even

know what she was waiting for. A miracle, perhaps. Orlandi didn't see it that way.

"Dear one, youth passes quickly. We've already loved each other for six useless years."

Teresina didn't understand the young man's discouraged tone. Why did he say they loved each other uselessly? Love is always love, she thought, and when you love you hope. She was still living with that tenuous thread of happiness. Why wasn't it enough for him?

It occurred to her to ask if he intended to continue writing newspaper articles all his life. But that boring subject would have taken the place of many kisses. And she wanted to hear other words from him: "my treasure, my life, my dear Teresa." All that was important; the rest faded away, lost in a distant fatalistic fog.

In the monotony of her life, her thoughts were her only moments of true happiness. She would feel like a woman, loved and loving. Then, as before, as always, for months she would be only the obedient daughter, the reserved girl, the good housewife.

"I'll probably settle in Milan."

"Yes?"

A sudden consternation appeared in Teresina's eyes. Milan was much further than Parma, and although she knew nothing of the big city, she vaguely guessed he would meet with greater temptations there. Her heart constricted with indefinable melancholy. All at once she got a glimpse of her humbleness, poverty, powerlessness. She yearned to tell him: Take me away! But the words died, strangled by a sob, and she could do no more than hide her face on his chest.

"See, see? I told you this life is impossible. I hate seeing you waste your youth. Teresa, my poor Teresa."

"Oh, call me yours, because I am yours."

She let herself go with such desperate abandon against his

chest that for an instant Orlandi's eyes flashed and he shook as if he had fever. But almost immediately, she loosened her grasp and nearly slid to the ground, where she stayed with her face in her hands, her body bent over.

Orlandi scrutinized that little virgin's head prostrated before him. "What do you intend to do?" he asked her in a gravely sweet tone, lifting her to her feet.

"Love you always, whatever happens, whatever my destiny."

He brought the girl's hand to his lips and placed there a hesitant, troubled kiss. Suddenly he had turned cool—affectionate, but distracted.

She didn't notice. She was still feeling his kisses, looking at him, touching him. It was impossible for her to think of anything else.

When Orlandi disappeared over the wall, Teresina was tempted to follow him. She wanted to shout, to call him, but turning suddenly as if she had heard a voice, she saw her house, her modest and austere house where her mother was resting, trusting in her. And she turned back with head bowed, unhappy with the rendezvous that had left her sadder than usual, with a discouragement deeper than her faith.

Chapter XIX

That year ended with two important events.

The younger Luminelli requested the hand of one of the twins, satisfied to take her without a dowry; and Carlino, graduating with a degree in law, left for a little town in southern Italy.

He had been advised to follow a judicial career, the most available, the surest way to allow him to give immediate aid to his family.

Signor Caccia depended a great deal on his son, for whom he and everyone in the family had made great sacrifices. Carlino had not become the eminent man his father had dreamed about when the little student spent hours reading in his study; nevertheless, after passing his exams and graduating like all the others, Carlino brought him a certain honor and sense of triumph that raised his eyebrows to greater heights than usual.

"Be careful," he told him as he departed, "never forget the good examples you got from your family. Be honest and firm."

And because Signora Soave was crying silently, sitting on the divan with her feet on a stool—so overcome she couldn't stand up—Signor Caccia looked her up and down and shook his thick shoulders. "It's awful being a woman," he thought, and turned to say good-bye to his son, stiff, unflappable, demonstrating his superiority.

Teresina was surprised at herself, and almost felt guilty for being so untouched by her brother's departure. Didn't she love him enough? No, that certainly wasn't it, but she was so absorbed in her love for that Orlandi that every other affection paled by comparison. And she had already suffered so much. Her heart no longer felt the sudden impulses of early youth; it was beginning to tire and had limits to the sorrow it could bear.

She had once reflected—not without reservations, afraid of being a bad sister—that if there hadn't been Carlino's education to support, the tax collector could have given her a small dowry. How this would have simplified everything!

She understood her father's reasons: she had lived in that environment and only that one for too long not to be convinced that her state as woman required resignation to her destiny—a destiny she was not free to direct, that she would have to accept as it came, stunted by family needs, subject to the needs and desires of others. Yes, she was convinced of all that. A blind man, convinced that he can no longer expect to see, might still ask the seeing world why he must be the victim.

When Carlino left with the hopes and best wishes of everyone, Teresina murmured sadly: "There he goes to make his future, as he wants, where he wants!"

So many sad thoughts came to haunt her that she found herself paralyzed at the moment of his departure. She appeared cold, indifferent. As soon as he left, she was filled with remorse. She always regretted every rebellious action. Under a veil of tears her face portrayed guilty anguish, along with terror, discomfort, unspeakable feelings.

Now she greatly resembled her mother, with that air of tired resignation. Signor Caccia dismissed them both in the same Olympic glance. Then he turned his eyes, slightly dilating with pleasure, on his pretty, robust Ida—festive even in the show of her regret.

Ida had the effect of a sunbeam on the family. She was everyone's beloved, their idol. From the day she was born, she had the gift of giving pleasure. Everyone indulged her. She was studying to be a teacher, and was already considered a prodigy.

After Ida, the twins held the most prominent place. It was impossible to ignore them—large, plump, ruddy, inseparable, resembling their father in their churlishness, wide shoulders, and bright coloring.

They assumed a commanding manner, with strength in their duplication: two voices, four eyes, four hands obedient to the one will between them.

Installed in Carlino's large room, they would stand at the window each morning to watch the passersby—fresh and bold in their twenties. Teresina now suffered from the cold, and in the morning, as soon as she got up, was too pale to let herself be seen at the window.

The twins had become close friends with the new renters of Calliope's house—the Ridolfis—who had two pretty girls. From one house to the other, looks, smiles, little gestures were continually telegraphed.

Teresina was excluded from this activity she didn't understand very well because, having spent her youth being mother to her sisters, she hadn't had time to find a friend her own age. She considered the judge's wife a faithful friend, but she was older, had growing girls and many preoccupations.

It hadn't been easy for Teresina to persuade her to receive Orlandi's letters in her name. These letters were unremarkable and arrived only occasionally, but Teresina opened them with pounding heart and read them avidly.

The judge's wife shook her head: it wasn't good to let things drag on so long. According to her, there was no longer a reason for continuing the correspondence.

But Teresina remembered their last meeting, the pure rapture, the true kisses. Ten months had gone by—ten months she hadn't seen Egidio—and yet memories of that night were constantly with her: the ball, his bold appearance, above all meeting him in the garden after a sleepless night on that cold February dawn.

She believed that Egidio would preserve his passion even at a distance, just as she did hers; and that no other woman could interest him, just as no man interested her.

Yet this naive faith was shaken at times. Looking around, reflecting, comparing, she saw and understood that everything in a young man's life was different than in a young woman's. It was logical that a man's love would not be the same as a woman's.

She also noticed a growing compassion for her among good people, a compassion that malicious people dressed in biting irony. Frequent allusions to girls who grow old at home, deprived of love, wounded her deeply.

Had she not loved? Had she not been loved? What was the mystery that had constantly eluded her, which seemed to command everyone's attention? What chain, what secret agreement bound men and women together who could understand each other with a monosyllable, a look? Love? She had loved. Could she love more than that?

As she lingered over this reflection, a slow blush rose to her cheeks. It was no longer the pervasive blush of fifteen—it was a reflex that barely warmed her skin before quickly subsiding to a natural pallor.

She was thinking: "No, it's not possible. Whatever love might be, it could not make me happier than I was, close in his arms that morning. At that moment, he was all mine."

Sometimes she tried to take her revenge on those contemptuous remarks of pity by replying arrogantly or not at all. Once the judge's wife said: "Don't act like that. They'll say you're becoming a bitter old maid." At such wounding words, Teresina shut herself in her room and wept as she had not wept since she was born.

She wept with the desperate tears of dying youth. She wept for herself, for her emaciated face, for her lackluster but once beautiful eyes, for her poor body once so full of life, now fossilizing. She was overwhelmed by despair, her body rocked with torrents of hate, wretched emotions, and envy such as she had never before felt.

She twisted in bed, biting her blanket with the insane desire to hurt someone, with the monstrous desire to see blood stream with her tears.

They found her unconscious, ashen, teeth clamped together.

Doctor Tavecchia, called in to calm her mother's fright, pronounced it nervous hysterics and prescribed tranquilizers.

From then on, the convulsions returned periodically. At first they were kept from her sisters, then accepted as a passing crisis, the result of a general weakening of her system. Doctor Tavecchia ordered iron pills.

Winter was taken up with preparing the bride's trousseau. It was done economically by sewing everything at home. Naturally, Teresina helped, and many times while she embroidered little scallops on the nightgowns, tears came to her eyes. One day, after working four hours straight, she said she was tired. Her eyes burned and everything looked blurred.

"If it were your trousseau you wouldn't be tired," the bride-to-be said cruelly.

Teresina bowed her head in silence. No one knew the effort it took not to slap her sister's face.

The fiancé, wildly in love, came every evening. He sat near his beloved and looked as though he wanted to eat her with his eyes. Kisses hovered on his lips, and every word that came out of them flew to her like a caress, warm with repressed ardor. It seemed as if his head, hands, knees were equipped with magnetic needles always turned to the same point, restrained only out of respect.

By tacit agreement, a space was left around the chairs of the couple. Signora Soave didn't move from her divan, surrounded by her three other daughters bent over their work, hurrying, diligent, responding briefly to their mother's complaints.

From the couple's corner in the shadows came subdued murmuring and broken sighs, all blended together in a joyous glow selfishly confined to the circle of the faint light. Until the arrival of Signor Caccia when the conversation became general.

Invariably at ten o'clock, the lamp was extinguished.

The two would say good night with a long handshake, gazing into each other's eyes, and closing her bedroom door, Teresina would sadly remember the times she waited for Egidio at the window after a boring evening.

Signor Caccia was thoroughly convinced his daughter had no more contact with Orlandi, whose continuing absence confirmed his conviction. And Teresina would rather have disappeared into the bowels of the earth than be caught for the third time.

For entire weeks she had to have patience, not daring to write often, always afraid the letters might go astray.

The judge's wife, who received Orlandi's letters for her, turned them over unwillingly. She would have preferred Orlandi not write anymore. In fact, she once decided to write him herself, begging him not to keep a hold on Teresa with vain hope.

The young man answered her evasively. He said he had already tried separation, realizing the possibility of marriage was too remote; however, Teresina did not agree and he didn't have the courage to be the first to leave.

The judge's wife tore up the letter: What great courage to stay a hundred miles away with every possible distraction and call it consoling!

With the trousseau as excuse, the Ridolfi girls gave the twins some fashion magazines to take home. Peeping out underneath these was a political journal of the elegant world. Teresina was interested in reading about opening nights and the balls she knew Egidio attended. The catalog of beautiful women, the description of their dresses, the excessive praise poisoned her blood.

One night she couldn't sleep because of this sentence: "Signora A., with her Junoesque shape arrayed artistically in an elegant huntress Diana costume, was accompanied by one of our most brilliant journalists, Signor O."

She couldn't be certain that O. meant Orlandi, but it still tortured her with jealousy. With a little imagination she managed to create the figure of Signora A., and she seemed to see her with her barely veiled Junoesque shape leaning on Egidio's arm.

The article describing the party added: "One cannot imagine anything more splendid except Armida's gardens. The flowers with their strong scents, wide velvet chalices, trembling corollas woven into festive garlands were hanging over the passing couples sweetly attracted by the exhilaration of the music, the fragrances, the dazzle of a thousand lights. And after the supper, when the longing to dance subsided for a few moments, the couples found sweet and voluptuous rest behind the plants next to every window and under the flowering azaleas, while the orchestra lulled them with Chopin's delicate nocturnes and Gounod's intoxicating serenade."

Closing her eyes, the poor martyr dreamed over and over with frightening clarity about all those splendors and luxuries of life. And he was enjoying them all!

Oh, those women who saw his smile, who took his hand, those women he held in his arms, who granted him the perfume of their beauty, how fortunate were those women near him!

Yet why did he go to the balls? Could he enjoy himself? Could he smile, embrace others? . . . She could never do it.

During the seven or eight hours he spent in those enchanting ballrooms, among the swish of satin and the sparkle of gems, did he ever think of her? He forgot her, then, for seven or eight hours. While she never forgot him for even one hour!

Milan became the tormenting locus of her thoughts. Every event taking place in that great city was of special interest to her. If it was about fights or injuries, she would always fear Egidio was involved. If it was about entertainment, suppers, theaters, she imagined he was there, and she would absorb the minutest details with a tormenting, jealous anxiety gnawing at her.

Often the newspaper brought news of the weather: "Today we had a splendid day," or "the rain threatens to last forever." Teresina's thoughts would run immediately to Egidio, following him down streets unknown to her, under sun or rain, keeping him company step by step.

Once someone said in her presence how likable the Milanese were, and it made Teresina unhappy. She felt a mute, profound displeasure that joined (as did her other displeasures) with a humiliating sense of powerlessness; and in the growing envy, the ferment in her dissatisfied heart so ill-treated by love, she felt the temptation of hate.

Then came the reaction, the contrition. She made her confession to God like a great sinner and, not wanting to blame anyone, she bowed deeply, weeping hot tears.

Chapter XX

Signora Soave hurried the wedding as much as possible because she felt the end of her life was near. She was dying as she had lived, accommodating, without terrible agonies, but with continuous, unremitting pain. Where was her suffering located? Nowhere and everywhere. It was a weakness, a general collapse. She was almost the same age as her husband and seemed more like his mother, the grandmother of his children.

With the windows open, she breathed the May air without moving from the divan, wrapped in a shawl, with her little wax hands crossed on her breast, her large dull eyes staring into space.

Teresina spent many hours at her side, while the twins relaxed in the garden and Ida did her homework.

The mysterious sympathy between mother and daughter made them more sensitive to each other's sadness, in that twofold deterioration of illusions and life. They never said much to one another, but from time to time their hands would seek the other's in a mute gentle clasp.

Signora Soave had never again spoken to Teresina about Orlandi. She had never asked her anything. Yet, looking into her mother's eyes, Teresina could read immense sympathy and infinite tenderness, made of forgiveness and love.

One evening her mother said to her: "Who will love you, Teresa, when I'm no longer here?"

Throwing herself into those loving arms, her daughter wanted to calm the dying woman's fears, she wanted to tell her that Egidio still loved her.

Signora Soave forestalled her, showing her with a sweet smile that she understood, and she added: "God keep you and guide you, my daughter." The only advice she offered was this: "Follow your heart."

Evening shadows darkening the room concealed her face, so Teresina couldn't see her expression of deep melancholy. Experience had taught the poor woman that the heart does not always lead to happiness, but like an ancient martyr, it dies for its faith.

Young Luminelli, who came punctually every day for his visit, was sometimes accompanied by his older brother, well received by the head of the house. They would talk politics together.

"If you had married him," the judge's wife said to Teresina, "you would already be married for ten years, prettier and fresher looking, and he wouldn't have become so ugly." Adding that since his daughter had died . . . he wasn't such a bad catch.

All these considerations didn't inspire the desired reformation in the spinster that her friend hoped for. To be polite Teresina had tried to get interested in him, in the good qualities everyone recognized. But his moral worth escaped her distracted attention, and instead she saw only the professor's bald head, his bristly beard cut like a myrtle bush. All this had an effect diametrically opposed to what her friend had in mind, because more than ever Teresina mourned Orlandi's beautiful black hair and his soft beard reflecting the playful sun.

"After all," her friend continued her incitements, "the years go by for Orlandi, too. Luzzi went to Milan not long ago and saw him. He says he isn't as handsome as he once was."

No matter what others did to try to make her forget Orlandi, it only ended by making her love him more. Teresina felt certain he was suffering, alone, without family, without love, and she wrote him a long letter overflowing with affection. How she yearned to see him! It had been almost a year and a half since she had held him against her heart. When would he come see her?

Egidio's feverish life, in the bitter, violent, everyday struggles of his frantic race for success, was not without its discouraging hours and dreadful melancholy. He found himself midway in life, his youth behind him, the best years lost, the strongest illusions vanished, without having made anything solid out of his talent, looks, or good health. Among themselves his friends said: Why hasn't Orlandi found a place for himself yet? One who knew him well defined him in a few words: Orlandi doesn't have the steadfastness of a good employee or the cleverness of an idle sponger. He's a failure at both.

This man whom fortune had falsely smiled upon, lavishing on him all its gifts, kept in the depths of his heart a sincere affection mixed with gratitude and pity for the girl who loved him so unselfishly.

His affection emerged especially strong on the miserable days when, after seeking new stimulations or indifferent friendships, after rejections or sensual nausea, he came home to letters from his poor forgotten love.

It was during one of these times that Egidio replied to Teresina, telling her of his misery, his struggles, calling her his sister, his friend.

"I understand," thought the judge's wife, seeing her friend's radiant face. "He's refilled the lamp with oil."

Another unexpected thing absorbed the whole family's attention. The older Luminelli asked for the hand of the other twin, and like something anticipated, the proposal was happily accepted. The two weddings were to take place on the same day.

"See?" said the judge's wife to Teresina. "Your sister is eight years younger than you, and yet she's settled on marrying him."

Teresina shrugged her shoulders. The twins had always been an enigma to her. She felt real repulsion for those loveless marriages. What infamous injustice still weighed on our society (which could be called uncivilized) when a girl was forced to choose between the absurdity of virginity or the shame of a marriage of convenience?

These reflections consumed her for several days, embittering her deeply. Unconsciously, she harbored innumerable misgivings, filling herself with resentments.

The collision of her feelings with brutal reality continued, making her unusually sharp. She herself realized she didn't fit in with the others. She heard her own surliness like a false note in a concert, but she was incapable of controlling it. All the more incapable because every day her contempt for others became rebellion against the hypocritical conventionality that had always oppressed her.

Her disgust for men took over slowly but completely.

Once the Ridolfis, referring to the youngest Portalupi, said: "Oh! She'll never marry. She's already an old maid."

The Portalupi girl was younger than Teresina.

She disliked all those girls, just as they disliked her. She kept to herself as much as possible, wrapped in a proud melancholy incomprehensible to those flighty young heads.

She had some fixations, some weird obsessions. When she went on a walk, she would never put her feet on the cracks between the bricks. If that happened inadvertently, she would feel a shiver run up her leg, a convulsive trembling. She counted the rosettes on the ceiling, imagining they were an even number. If they turned out to be odd, it made her cross and angry—absurd, but she couldn't help it. She would stare at someone's back relentlessly until they turned around. If they didn't turn it was like a blow to the chest, making her teeth grind.

She was bothered by the sun, wind, rainy weather. Her upper arms were always chilly, and under her dress she wore two woolen sleeves connected by a ribbon that crossed her back.

If the twins cut out a sleeveless shirt, they would say laughingly: "This would be good for Teresina!"

Without having the care of her sisters, which had occupied her in the past, her days were empty. She wasn't even able to help Ida, because she had never been very clever in school and the girl was very quick. Ida was already ahead in her studies, dreaming of a teacher's certificate.

Her brother was too far away and offered no financial help. Yet they spoke of him as the only salvation of the family's future. When the twins were married, she could join him to form a household together or be the reason why he should transfer to his native town.

In anticipation of these changes, in the bustle of the weddings, with her horror of the world and society, Teresina lived almost exclusively in the company of her ill mother—both protected from the breezes with their feet on the same stool, smiling sadly.

A desperate thought seized her from time to time. She was afraid of becoming an old eccentric like Calliope, shutting herself up in the house to be seen only at the barred windows, with a yellow kerchief on her head, making faces at those passing by.

No matter how fast everyone worked, the double wedding couldn't take place before the first of September. On that day, Teresina had one of her attacks. Ida put her to bed lovingly, trying to calm her, remembering how patient Teresina had been with her when she was small.

Teresa didn't attend the ceremony or the reception.

After the wedding, the twins came to see her, holding up the flounces of their dresses. They were in a hurry to catch the train and didn't sit down. At the doorway they turned; they had forgotten to kiss her and so threw a little kiss from their fingertips, telling her to stay calm and quiet.

Little by little, the house returned to normal. The fashion illustrations, the rolls of linen, the little pieces of ribbon lying forgotten on the furniture disappeared. A tomblike silence replaced the twins' noisy shouting and the Ridolfi girls' silvery laughter.

In his study Signor Caccia brooded over the expenses incurred by the weddings and turned his thoughts to his far-away son, the one who had to be the family's support.

Ida studied tirelessly without distractions, her eyes on her goal.

Only toward evening would Ida leave her books and Teresa leave her mother's bedside. Then the two sisters—the oldest and the youngest—would go out to take the air, both solemn for different reasons, exchanging few words.

At the end of September, Ida sprained her ankle and couldn't go out for a week. Since the doctor had vigorously advised Teresina to walk every day, she went out alone. She was now more than thirty years old and no one paid attention to her anymore.

These preludes to freedom, even though they came at a time when she wouldn't know how to take advantage of them, brought about a new pleasure. She walked out of town on the road to Madonna della Fontana, dear to her because of old memories; and passing again under the trees, she was overcome by so many sweet and sad emotions—so vivid, so intense—that that evening walk signaled the most beautiful time of her day.

One evening she entered the church to see the underground chapel again, the lovely little painted chapel whose windows looked out on the curate's garden perfumed with basil.

Bitter, pungent memories of her youth besieged her there, where she had knelt at twenty, where she had seen Egidio for the first time. Sprigs of basil were still beyond the window, roses were dying on the altar between silver-plated lamps, the delicately painted figures of the fresco were still smiling. Nothing had changed in the great, still calm of the temple; Teresina wept.

The sound of echoing footsteps in the silence of the nave above brought her to herself. She dried her eyes with the corner of her veil and went out of the chapel. In the middle of the church she saw Orlandi, alone, coming toward her.

She wasn't even surprised, although she grew pale, grabbing at his arm, her teeth chattering from emotion.

"When did you get here?"

"Two hours ago. A telegram from my aunt . . . about business. I must return tonight."

"And you weren't going to see me?"

"I'm seeing you now," Orlandi said with his beautiful smile. "I didn't have time to let you know, but I decided to see you at any cost. By chance I found out you were here. My aunt saw you go by."

Teresina didn't give a thought to the danger of being discovered. The happiness of the moment totally enveloped her. However, the shock was too much in her weakened state, and she was unable to stand. She dragged Egidio to a church pew and sat down beside him, oblivious to the whole world, as she always was in his presence.

They spoke rapidly about their families, about their own situation.

Looking at him in the dying light, Teresina felt a pain in her heart at the sight of the two furrows on his cheeks, which gave his beautiful face an expression of indefinable melancholy.

"Do you find me changed?" he said suddenly, and with a sad smile showed her his thinning hair.

She pulled him close to her until her mouth was on his chest, murmuring: "And me?"

They sat silently in that near embrace, listening to their breathing, able to kiss but not doing so.

"You write so seldom . . ." she said in a low voice, looking at him sweetly to soften the reprimand.

He passed a hand over his forehead. "I'm busy every day and most evenings."

"Where do you go in the evening?"

"First to the theater, then to the newspaper office. I do the news. I don't like that. I'd rather be an art critic."

"And you can't be?"

"No . . . no . . . these are things you don't understand."

Teresina lowered her head in humility at her own ignorance and the discomfort of being unable to share all his thoughts and pain. The image of the beautiful signora with the opulent shape, dressed like Diana, flashed through her mind, but she didn't have the courage to mention it at that moment.

It always happened like this. She could never tell him one of the thousand things she wanted to, dominated by a strange fear and so totally absorbed in looking at him.

The sorrow, anxieties, struggles, jealousies, resolutions made and rejected, the convulsive ecstasies, the hysterical melancholia, her whole youth, beauty, life disappearing in that slow flame of love didn't offer a single word. She remained quiet beside him, with her eyes staring like a faithful dog with its master.

"They'll be expecting you at home . . ."

"Oh, just another minute . . ."

She was wondering if she didn't have something else to tell him, but couldn't think of a thing. She would have liked to know something about him and his life; she would have liked for him to talk, but didn't dare press him, afraid of losing time with idle questions.

In the meanwhile, time was passing.

It grew dark in the church. Immersed in shadow, the main altar looked vaguely like a casket, the columns of the nave like gigantic phantoms. From the underground chapel came the reddish reflection of the lamp burning for the Madonna. An odor of dry roses was in the air.

In the sacristy, the sexton shook his bundle of keys. They rose together, bumping into each other in the darkness. Egidio took her by the waist.

"Oh!" she said. "If only they would close us up in here forever; we would see no one and could die like this."

Their lips joined.

He was amazed by that burning poetic thought. Supporting her as they left the church, he murmured in her ear: "When I feel like dying, I'll come die with you."

They said no more, holding each other in a long, desperate embrace. Teresa disappeared quickly through the trees. Egidio escorted her from a distance as far as town.

Chapter XXI

A few months after the twins' wedding, Signora Soave closed her eyes in peace.

In mourning her, Teresina realized her greatest comfort, most unconditional source of love, was gone; perhaps of the whole family only she felt the emptiness left by her death.

For Signor Caccia it was a relief. With the egoism of a robust man, he thought the poor woman should have died much sooner. Now that his family was smaller, he could embrace more than ever his lifelong dream: to push his son rapidly ahead in his career, make him head of the household, put his beleaguered finances back in shape, and after five or six years of the strictest economy, get him a brilliant match, a beautiful wife, and a rich dowry.

In these future dispositions, Ida, his favorite after his son, had her future secured as schoolmistress. As for Teresa, seeing her go around the house, wasting away, with her dark eyes devoid of any splendor, with her little hands the color of wax, he was convinced she would never do more than her mother, and his wide shoulders slumped in contempt.

She had to hide her suffering to avoid his rebukes, and yet this suffering increased with every passing day.

She was unable to eat anymore at the usual hour. Food eaten in company made her ill; therefore, she ate leftovers alone in the kitchen.

Many times, in her calmest moments, working quietly along-side her sister, she would start shouting: "It's coming! It's coming!" (meaning the illness), and with a hand on her stomach, her eyes wide open, her mouth foaming as though she had seen a horrible monster, she would go into the early stage of convulsions. She said they pinched her chest. That was the way she described it.

Tranquilizers were useless; she refused them in horror, complaining they made her ill, motioning with her arms for those around her to move away so she could breathe.

During these attacks, beads of sweat formed on her forehead and her teeth chattered. Her hands and feet were like ice. If the convulsion was strong delirium would follow, accompanied by nervous shaking, shouts, weak moans, and groans so agonizing she seemed at the point of death.

Then they had to lay her on her bed in absolute silence until the attack passed and she fell into deep sleep from which she would awake remembering nothing.

When there was no delirium, the convulsion would end in a fit of weeping; however, this made a deeper impression on her and almost always ended in a melancholy lasting many days.

On the night table beside her bed was a neat row of bottles and cruets: water with chamomile, antihysteria pills, iron pills, arsenic drops, vinegar, orange blossoms, lemon balm. The drawer contained roasted coffee beans she chewed when awake, something the doctor had warned her against.

But Tavecchia, who was more than seventy, didn't want to assume all the responsibility for this nervous malady and suggested a young doctor instructed in modern theories, and versed in pathology as well as psychiatry.

One day the young doctor came and said he wanted to check the patient to be sure of the diagnosis.

Teresina didn't get up the next day, agitated by the prospect of that visit and opposed to it.

"Put on a pretty cap," Ida said, laughing, to distract her.

She didn't want the cap; in fact, she removed the kerchief she usually wore, ashamed of being seen with her head covered like an old woman.

She still had beautifully long, soft hair. Looking at herself in the mirror Ida handed her, she was satisfied. The white frame of the pillow delicately emphasized her small head. The warmth of the bed put a rosy shine on her cheeks and her face lost its ascetic thinness. Her slightly pale mouth was surrounded by some lines, but when she smiled her finely shaped lips revealed white teeth.

"What will he make me do?" she asked her sister while assuring herself the top button of her nightgown was fastened.

"Nothing . . . he'll order more pills for you. You don't have a disease. Don't be afraid."

"Oh, I'm not afraid of that! Please stay here and don't leave me alone."

When the doctor came, Teresa was in such a state of excitement she had to be given some drops of lemon balm to soothe her.

Ida, who understood nothing of the multitude of symptoms that seemed imaginary to her, stood beside the bed watching the doctor. Signor Caccia, grumpy and severe, waited.

The examination was long and detailed. It began with a number of questions, some of which were unexpected and others incomprehensible to the sick woman, who was content to bow her head mutely as if tormented by a nightmare.

At a certain point, the doctor pulled back the blanket. "Sit up, but please stay calm."

She was truly dazed, trembling, her forehead covered in sweat.

"I can't examine her in this condition," the doctor said, stepping back.

Signor Caccia intervened, speaking loudly and looking at his daughter crossly.

"No, no," the doctor said. "It makes it worse to criticize her. Let's let her recover gently. That makes sense, doesn't it?"

He sat beside the bed smiling, calm, looking intently at Teresa.

Signor Caccia started to walk impatiently about the room, then, outside the door, letting them hear the dry cough of a man restraining himself.

The doctor remained alone between the two sisters, turning his back slightly to Ida, completely involved with the patient.

Teresa felt that look penetrate her body and thoughts. She didn't look at him, but even avoiding his gaze, she felt its intensity. In this way she grew even more strongly aware of it until, attracted by an overpowering magnetism, she returned his gaze. In this stillness, she became suddenly calm.

Then the doctor gently lifted her hand and took her pulse. "Good." He stood up and invited her to sit up again as she had before.

Ida started to call her father, but the doctor stopped her with a gesture while he bent over Teresina to put his ear to her heart.

In the silence of the room the breathing of all three could be heard.

"That's enough," the patient murmured almost immediately.

"Am I hurting you?"

She didn't answer, but fell back palely on the pillows.

The doctor pursed his lips.

"Let me . . . be patient."

Again he laid his head on her heart, pressing lightly.

He had a forest of thick brown hair that gave off a faint perfume. Displaced by his motion, his hair fell almost to Teresina's mouth; she stiffened, her eyes dilating under the temptation of a crazy desire. His ears, the roots of his hair, his throat were faintly pink, the back of his neck snow white. He was twenty-nine years old.

"Nothing. Nothing wrong with her heart . . . physically."

This last word was emphasized by a slight hesitation as he straightened up, a little red in the face.

At this point, Signor Caccia reentered the room.

"Your daughter has a very good constitution. Sound lungs, healthy heart. A tendency toward anemia, perhaps, but this is temporary, dependent on causes that this examination doesn't show."

"But if you saw her during these attacks, when she has convulsions . . . You can't imagine."

"Oh, yes. I can imagine perfectly," the doctor said with a smile. "But it's nothing more than an alteration in her nervous system. With time and a little goodwill, I think it'll go away."

While saying "goodwill" he turned to look at Teresa. "You don't stay in the house too much, do you?"

"But . . . really," stammered Signor Caccia. "Women . . ."

The doctor continued without letting him finish: "With such a strong nervous disturbance, of a definite hysterical nature, the best cure is not to leave the patient alone. I can prescribe some medicine, but if it isn't helped by the routine . . ." He looked directly at Teresa. "The weather is favorable, we're having an enchanting spring. Go out often. Go visit a friend, get interested in something that will take you out of your routine thoughts, so as not to fix on one idea. I recommend a little arsenic and iron; but the best remedy, I'm convinced, you must find in yourself. You understand me, don't you?"

He shook her hand with the sweet indolence of a secure man, showing white teeth in the arc of his smile, leaving the perfume of his vigorous youth at her bedside.

A few days later, he returned to check on the results of his suggestions. When he suddenly appeared, Teresina blushed in confusion with a secret feeling of shame.

That sort of intimacy with a young man without the bond of love disturbed her. She was amazed at not feeling greater aversion to the contact, surprised to find an autonomous life in her senses, independent of her heart and will.

Up to now she had loved the incarnation of love in one man alone. Her heart and mind had withstood the straining of her whole being toward that ideal, but not her nerves. Without her conscious awareness, her nerves vibrated fiendishly when the young doctor shook her hand and looked at her intensely. Teresa suffered agonies, feeling in her throat a kind of convulsive death rattle, finding in the tardy revelation of her own senses the enigma of life that had sporadically appeared to her in a concealed and distorted form, kept hidden like something shameful.

By chance she came upon one of the old books her father had bought. The title inspired her to read the first page, and as she kept reading in anxious amazement, she passed from surprise to indignation to fierce pleasure to the most repugnant nausea.

She remained immobile, blood pounding in her veins, cheeks flaming, her jaws jutting forward, her eyes glassy.

Never had she heard or imagined anything like it.

When she came to herself, indignation overcame every other feeling. She ripped the book into a thousand pieces, tearing each piece smaller and smaller; finally, she tasted a purifying joy by stomping on them. Then she gathered up the pieces and threw them into the rubbish bin. But they could be seen. Their filthy whiteness stood out against the black background. That wasn't what she wanted. She fished them out and burned them—alive— because those fragments agitated by the flames gave her the impression of live things, obscene monsters condemned to the stake.

At last a pile of ashes convinced her there was nothing left of that filth.

But she was deceiving herself. Her thoughts were affected, unalterably stained. As much as she tried, she couldn't remove the memory of the pages she had read, a bitter memory, like medicine that won't go down.

And unsought came the reflections, the comparisons, the realizations. A hundred things that had remained obscure up to that time became piteously clear. She no longer had uncertainties, and all self-delusion was over.

Those cruel explanations were the only answer she had found to her long unsatisfied curiosity.

Those printed pages that didn't fly away like words, didn't vanish like smiles, that she had destroyed one example of, but that existed in a thousand others, those infamous pages were a document of human misery, of her own misery.

A filthy book had given her the key to the mystery she had sought in vain, that she had questioned in her own frightening, prudish thrills, in the malicious reticence of others.

Was this, then, the despicable secret that held men and women together? This was love?

Subtly, profoundly, one thought above all tormented her: Egidio. When his image became mixed with lascivious thoughts, she felt the greatest shame of her life. Everything sacred to her in the world seemed to be dragged through mud. It was a profanation of the most gentle affection, the shattered altar, the idol become clay.

And she was as overcome by sorrow and sadness as if she had lost a loved one forever. For the entire day she was unable to look anyone in the face; she was horrified by her kind.

In the evening, she shut herself in her room with the illusion she was getting away from that nightmare. But it became even more violent.

While she undressed she was assailed by a brutal curiosity. It was as if the infamous pages were glued to her skin, forming a sheath of flame like the shirt of Nessus, in which she struggled.

In desperation she fell on her knees, mechanically reciting every prayer she knew, joining Egidio's name with the Madonna's, in the frenzied need to forget.

Lying exhausted under the covers, she evoked the pure visions of her love: the meeting in the chapel, the rendezvous in church, the first appointment at the window under the driving rain that neither of them heard, and those heavenly, soul-felt kisses.

Gradually a sense of peace enveloped her. A melancholy sweetness lulled and consoled her. Egidio had always been honest. He had never deceived nor betrayed her. He had never pretended to be something he wasn't. What more could you ask of a man?

Now she felt an extraordinary, tender longing to pity him, to understand him in the weakness of his sex. The recent outrage had made her heart bleed, but from that wound itself rose her most noble ideals to reach a pious compassion, a commiseration with this suffering, bestial humanity, a graceful impulse to forgive. Her affection, which she knew to be divided, emerged stronger and purer from so much mud.

Softly sighing, she closed her eyes in resignation.

From time to time a chill still shook her, but that eventually disappeared in the drowsy warmth, until her quiet breathing indicated her thoughts had fallen asleep.

Chapter XXII

The ground was dry, scorched by the sun beating down on it all day. The pitiful little plants in the garden lost their leaves. Flowers, bending over their stems, apparently lacked the strength to be fragrant. In the corner of a flower bed, a night geranium was beginning to open its calyx of faded colors and intoxicating scent.

Teresina had been caring for this very unusual flower for a short time, but she had a special interest in it. Amazed and gratified by something so ugly and so sweet smelling, and so modest it never opened before sunset.

She had come from the house with a watering can, as tired and exhausted as her flowers, feeling the weight of the intolerable heat of that July day. She stopped a moment to look around, already dreading the fatigue of watering.

In sorrowful resignation, she slowly rolled up the cuff of her sleeves, first the left and then the right, exposing the beginning of her thin arms without looking at them.

The old yellow dress she was wearing didn't become her—she knew it but didn't care. She hated clothes and fashion.

However, she was not yet ugly. Her pretty face that suffering had made thin but not unattractive lacked only a ray of happiness. Like all sunsets, it needed a bright sky to be beautiful.

This passion for flowers had come to her only recently, and Teresa had welcomed it as a relief from her near total isolation.

For six months, her father had been confined to an armchair. That colossus had been struck by an attack of apoplexy that paralyzed his legs and hands. She had to dress and undress him, put him to bed, feed him just like a child. She never left the house anymore since she had been left alone—Ida had obtained a teaching position in southern Italy—and from that time, people said, the tax collector had begun to fret and lose his health.

Almost every evening the doctor, who had become a friend, came to spend half an hour with the patient. Teresina took advantage of that half hour to go into the garden.

"Aren't you through yet?" the doctor's fresh, virile voice shouted from the porch.

"It was so hot today, they're thirsty," Teresa replied without looking up.

He came over to look at the flowers and said: "It might rain."

His closeness made Teresina hurriedly roll down her sleeves. "Maybe rain's not far off."

They both looked at the sky. Teresa rested the watering can on the path and stood still, her arms at her side, with a tired expression that made her face look thinner.

From the dampened flower beds the smell of cool, sharp, sensual earth began to rise, cutting the dryness of the atmosphere. Everything in the ground—little worms and caterpillars—was revitalized by those few drops of water.

Although the air was scorching, a soft breeze moved slowly through it like a caress.

"Isn't that a nice smell?"

She said yes distractedly, feeling the irresistible need to live penetrate every pore. Her apathy was misleading.

She watched the ground soak up the water and the flowers swell up and rise from the sod.

The doctor was talking with that male voice that made Teresina tremble. Her thoughts were far away, but the usual magnetic current, purely physical, kept her listening to the young man. With her eyes lowered, she could obliquely see the slow movement of his long brown mustache throw a shadow on the solid whiteness of his chin.

She was thinking, "If only he were here!" It joined the soul of the absent one to the material sensations of the moment.

Perhaps the doctor was feeling something similar: bodily present, his thoughts were far away. His eyes stared like someone seeing a vision, and he traced some incomprehensible letters in the sand with his cane. Without quite knowing how it came about, he began speaking about love:

"In plays and novels of the past we often meet this situation: a woman falls in a pond, a man saves her, they fall in love. Why? What do they know about each other? Have they tried to understand each other in the long silences where the heart speaks? Have they laughed and cried together? Do they only know how they eat and sleep? In what way is their spirit exhilarated and to what point do their nerves thrill? Beauty that wounds rarely lasts. True love is born from a whole set of circumstances, of infinite and continuous affinities. It's a certain way of looking, of feeling, of expressing ideas; it's a contour of the lip, the voice, gestures, the shape of the hands, the odor of the skin. It's the prolonged attraction of their bodies, when the closer they are the closer they want to be. It's the quick and total exchange of thoughts; it's the binding of the same feeling, the merging, the completion of both in a progressive absorption of mind and senses . . ."

"That's true, that's true."

With her eyes closed, leaning against the trunk of a little tree, Teresa murmured again: "That's true." She felt lulled by that voice, almost asleep in her eternal song of love, while the ground around her sent up strong, wild exhalations and the flowers straightened up luxuriantly, and the grass, leaves, every stem, every bush gave off sweet smells in the damp coolness of the evening, beaded with the recent drops of water.

". . . Love is the look that flies swift as a dart, it's the word that the lip barely utters, it's the desire that emotion paralyzes . . ."

"That's true, that's true."

She thought she might die in a rapture of sensual pleasure, in the delicate excitement of that man's voice speaking of love.

Abruptly, the young man stopped.

Night had descended, fresh, sweet, full of soft breezes. The first stars shone in the sky. The intense perfume of the night geranium was sweet, almost carnal, as it stretched its branches toward the silvery light. In that silence the droplets lapped the petals, trickled down the stems, dropped on the ground with a dull little sound that disturbed the flies in their first sleep and made the glowworms dart timorously from flower to flower.

When the young man began to speak again, his voice had changed. He said good evening hurriedly, without looking at her, grasping a thought that had come to him in the tempting sweetness of that night. He disappeared in the shadows of the porch.

Teresa shook herself, gritted her teeth, closed her eyes, and sighed. Raising her arms over her head, she stretched them with an abandon to which her whole body responded with a moan.

Signor Caccia was ending his days in the women's damp, dark parlor, confined to the uncomfortable divan where Signora Soave had spent such a large part of her life complaining sweetly with her eyes turned heavenward.

He had ended up a beaten man, his great strength defeated, reduced to the wretched state of having to rely on the pity of others, stripped of every power, at the mercy of the only daughter remaining with him.

And she was not his favorite daughter; in fact, he had often disowned her, making her the victim of his absolutism. Now they were faced with each other, alone, with all the past separating them, with indestructible bitterness for the pain suffered. They didn't speak, but in the daughter's silence there was perhaps a reprimand; in the father's silence perhaps a sense of remorse for his arrogance, and humiliation at his obligation to her for his continued existence.

Sometimes he watched her in dull anger. At other times with a sudden impulse of tenderness.

Teresa was calm. She made no exaggerated displays of affection, but was attentive and docile. She fulfilled her obligations without enthusiasm and without excessive weariness.

Her whole faded youth remained in the house around her, within those walls that had seen her as a child; where every day, every hour a particle of her beauty had fallen like sand in an hour glass; where she had watched the succession of years go by in the family's and her own slow evolution.

She looked back on the past as though she were looking at someone else, recalling Teresina at fifteen—so happy the day she left for Marcaria on the long sunny road that went on forever, where Orlandi's buggy traveled in a cloud of dust. Thinking back over it, it seemed a prophecy: he passed her by on the run.

Oh, how she would have liked to start her life over now that she understood more.

Assailed by this thought, she struggled in profound melancholy, with spiteful envy coloring everything, with ancient regrets, with jealously guarded desires she had thought vanquished forever.

They passed long, painful hours like this, father and daughter—always united, dignified, fiercely supporting the burden of their duty, dragging the odious chain of habit, of imposed affections.

A letter from Carlino brought the final blow to those two who still represented the Caccia family. The young man briefly announced his marriage to an innkeeper's daughter he had seduced. Not a word of apology, no deference to paternal authority. Nothing. It was the brutal will of a free man who needed no one.

Signor Caccia was pitifully shaken. The doctor, who came when the sick man's condition worsened, said he would not recover from that blow.

In fact, he continued to grow worse, and at the beginning of autumn, after losing his faculty of speech and memory, he had a heart attack and died.

Everyone in town thought Teresina would go live with her married sisters, but Teresina didn't move.

She stayed with her father until his last breath, prepared him for the bier, watched over his body. The moment they took him away, she cried. Then she took up her tranquil routine again, wandering around like a phantom in the deserted house.

In vain everyone—the doctor, the judge's wife, the Ridolfi neighbors—tried to get her to go out, to have some diversion. She refused all their suggestions so calmly and coldly they all decided she was emotionally frozen.

"Poor little thing!" thought the judge's wife. "She's suffered so much her heart has hardened; she doesn't feel anything."

Yet, as an extreme recourse, justified by long friendship, one day the judge's wife tried to appeal to Teresina's ego, and said: "I'm afraid you really do resemble Calliope; you never go out, you keep the house barred . . . see if you can make faces at me."

Even here Teresina was invulnerable. A serious, profoundly sad smile was her answer to everything and everyone.

Two months went by.

Toward the last days of the year, she received a letter from Egidio. He was sick, poor, and without any help. He wrote her as a son would write his mother, with unlimited faith.

Teresa thought about this letter for some time and didn't sleep all night. The next day she thought about it some more.

The judge's wife, after not seeing her for a while, stopped by for a visit. She found her in her room surrounded by clothes, with objects tossed helter-skelter around on the furniture, her traveling bag open on the floor.

"What's this I see? You've finally decided to go live with the Luminellis?"

Teresa didn't reply immediately. She was very preoccupied, but after a moment took her friend's hand and spoke softly, seriously: "He wrote me."

The judge's wife didn't understand at once. For six or seven months they had not mentioned Orlandi's name. Therefore she didn't hide her surprise—quite the opposite: "He wrote to you again? What does he want?"

"Nothing."

The judge's wife shook her head. Teresina added: "He's sick."

"Oh!"

"Alone."

This time the judge's wife didn't say a word. A brief, thoughtful silence followed.

Teresa folded a dress on the bed, turning her back to her friend. Quickly, the way a tooth is pulled, she said: "I'm leaving tomorrow."

She turned with the dress on her arm. The two women exchanged glances. The judge's wife understood.

She was quiet while Teresa packed her bag. When she was finished, they sat down on the bed simultaneously, serious and profoundly moved.

"Have you thought about this?"

"Yes."

"And you've made up your mind?"

"I've made up my mind."

The judge's wife attempted sarcasm, saying with a cold smile: "You're going to be a nurse!"

"Whatever God wills," was Teresa's reply.

The other continued: "What will your sisters think, your brother?"

She shrugged her shoulders.

"The people?"

"Oh, the people . . ." And she smiled her melancholy smile traced with irony.

"Nevertheless, if someone says something to me, your friend?"

"Well, you can tell those zealous people I've paid my whole life for this moment of freedom. That price is high enough, don't you agree?"

She smiled again and smoothed her lackluster hair with her two little hands of yellow wax.

The judge's wife stayed with her most of the day.

The next morning, dressed in mourning black, a veil hiding half her face, Teresa closed the door of her house.

Her friend, faithful to the last moment, was with her. "We'll see each other again, you know."

"Let's hope so," replied Teresa gravely, all too aware of the mysteries of the future.

Don Giovanni Boccabadati, wrapped in a fur coat, put his head out the window. Teresa remembered the day he had left with the sun and bird song one spring morning.

"It's not good weather for you," the judge's wife said.

Teresa casually glanced up at the sky and set out with her friend for the station.

Before entering the waiting room, they stopped again to exchange farewell wishes and renew their requests for the other to write.

As Teresa was leaving the room after showing her ticket, her friend grabbed her for a last embrace. She wanted to tell her something, but emotion made her mute. They exchanged intense looks without another word.

"All aboard! All aboard!"

The judge's wife ran to the gate to see her friend one last time. They saluted each other with hands and eyes as long as possible. Then Teresa's black veil stopped fluttering at the window and the train moved out of sight just as the first snow began to fall.

European Classics

M. Ageyev
Novel with Cocaine

Jerzy Andrzejewski
Ashes and Diamonds

Honoré de Balzac
The Bureaucrats

Andrei Bely
Kotik Letaev

Heinrich Böll
Absent without Leave
And Never Said a Word
And Where Were You, Adam?
The Bread of Those Early Years
End of a Mission
Irish Journal
Missing Persons and Other Essays
The Safety Net
A Soldier's Legacy
The Stories of Heinrich Böll
Tomorrow and Yesterday
The Train Was on Time
What's to Become of the Boy?
Women in a River Landscape

Madeleine Bourdouxhe
La Femme de Gilles

Karel Čapek
Nine Fairy Tales
War with the Newts

Lydia Chukovskaya
Sofia Petrovna

Grazia Deledda
After the Divorce
Elias Portolu

Leonid Dobychin
The Town of N

Yury Dombrovsky
The Keeper of Antiquities

Aleksandr Druzhinin
Polinka Saks • The Story
 of Aleksei Dmitrich

Venedikt Erofeev
Moscow to the End of the Line

Konstantin Fedin
Cities and Years

Arne Garborg
Weary Men

Fyodor Vasilievich Gladkov
Cement

I. Grekova
The Ship of Widows

Vasily Grossman
Forever Flowing

Stefan Heym
The King David Report

Marek Hlasko
The Eighth Day of the Week

Bohumil Hrabal
Closely Watched Trains

Ilf and Petrov
The Twelve Chairs

Vsevolod Ivanov
Fertility and Other Stories

Erich Kästner
Fabian: The Story of a Moralist